THE MIRR

Catherine Storr was born and lived most of her life in London, apart from some years in Cambridge, where she took a degree first in English Literature and then in Medicine. She then practised medicine for fifteen years, but never forgot her other ambition – to be a writer. She wrote her first children's books for her three daughters. Her classic collection of stories *Clever Polly and the Stupid Wolf* was written for a small Polly who was scared of the wolf under her bed. Other novels for children followed, including the powerful *Marianne Dreams*, which was filmed as *The Paper House* in 1990. Now that her daughters are grown up, Catherine Storr sometimes writes for adults, but she is sure that she will always want to write for children because they share her enjoyment of a story and understand that fantasy and reality are not opposites – but different ways of looking at the same thing.

The Mirror Image Ghost

CATHERINE STORR

faber and faber

First published in 1994
First published in paperback in 1995
Reset and published in this paperback edition in 2000
by Faber and Faber Limited
3 Queen Square London WC1N 3AU

Photoset by Avon Dataset Ltd, Bidford on Avon
Printed in England by Mackays of Chatham plc, Chatham, Kent

A CIP record for this book is available from the British Library

ISBN 0–571–20217–9

2 4 6 8 10 9 7 5 3 1

The Mirror Image Ghost

The mirror hung in Fanny's room, opposite the windows which looked out on to the small London gardens at the back of the house. Now the mirror reflected light: the morning sun, the English sky, often streaked with clouds, the scanty, pale modern English furniture of Fanny's bedroom.

It was not an English mirror. It had been made in Germany, nearly two hundred years before. It had a heavy frame of dark, carved wood, and it was long enough to show the reflection of a grown person, full length. Now the person it showed most often was Fanny; but in its long history, it had shown a great many people doing many different things. It had shown people being born, growing up and dying. It had shown people laughing and crying, loving and quarrelling, eating, drinking, celebrating, praying. There was nothing that people do, whether kind or hateful, comforting or terrifying, which the mirror had not seen and reflected in its time.

But it was silent about these memories. It did not tell what it had seen. It held all this within its silvered glass and the wooden frame. Perhaps it could have spoken only to another mirror. A mirror like the little hand looking-glass which lay just in front of it, on Fanny's dressing-table. It would not be until the two mirrors were placed so that each reflected the other that any of their secrets could be told. And this did not happen until Lisa . . .

But this is the beginning of Lisa's story and must be told in the right order in a new chapter.

'Have you ever seen a ghost, Grandma?' Lisa asked.

'What's put you on to ghosts?' her grandmother said.

'Been reading.'

'Ghost stories? Frightening?'

'Some of them are. Most aren't. Just . . .' She looked for the right word.

'Eerie?'

'What's that mean?'

'Means . . . strange. Not sure what's real and what isn't. As if there might be another world you can't quite see or hear, but you think might be there. All round you.'

Lisa tried the word out. 'Eerie. Did you ever feel like that?'

'Not often. John says I'm too matter-of-fact to have feelings I can't explain.'

'Has Grandpa seen a ghost, then?'

'He's not sure. Any more than I am.'

'You mean you did see something? Both of you? Together?'

'Lisa! Go and wash your hands before supper.'

'But I want to know what you saw.'

'Another time,' her grandmother said.

'Please, now!'

When her grandmother said, 'No,' in that special voice, there was no appeal. Lisa washed her hands and joined her grandparents in the kitchen. She'd meant to tackle them at once about ghosts, but the subject was driven out of her mind by her grandfather's first remark.

'Peter is almost exactly your age, isn't he?'

'He doesn't like being called Peter. He says his name is Pierre,' Lisa said.

'Peter . . . Pierre, they're the same thing. His age is the same, whatever you call him. Eleven, isn't he? The same as you?'

Lisa said, 'No, he's twelve. Just.'

'And the girl? How old is she?'

'She's ten.'

'I can't remember her name.'

'Alice. She calls it Aleese.'

'That's the French pronunciation,' Lisa's grandmother said.

'I think it sounds silly,' Lisa said.

Lisa's grandfather ate for a time in silence. Then he said, 'Why don't you like Pierre?'

'He's horrible,' Lisa said.

'Teases you?'

'Sort of. He and Alice talk French to each other so that I can't understand.'

'It is their mother tongue.'

'Their what? You mean because their mother is French?'

'Mother tongue means the language you learn when you are a baby. Your first language. As mine was German. I suppose they can speak English too?'

'Yes. That's why it's so mean of them to talk French when I'm there.'

'You could always learn it,' Grandpa said.

'Don't want to. It sounds silly.'

'It is silly to be so prejudiced,' Grandpa said.

'How do they behave to your mother?' Grandma asked.

'They're not so bad when she's there. Laurent won't let them be horrible to her.'

'Do you get on all right with him?' Grandpa asked.

'I don't see him that much. He's out all day.' Her voice said what her words didn't: 'Thank goodness, I don't want him around.'

'He makes your mother happy,' Grandpa said, in the voice he sometimes used when he didn't like the last thing that had been said. If she had been with anyone except Grandpa, Lisa would have said, 'He doesn't make me happy.'

After they'd cleared the table, Lisa and her grandmother walked round the garden to decide what the next day's jobs were to be. At first Grandma didn't talk about anything except the weeds that must be cleared and the chrysanthemums which should be tied. She warned Lisa not to get mulberry juice on her clothes because it was impossible to wash out. But under the Ribstone Pippin tree, she stopped and said, 'Is there anything else besides them talking to each other in French?'

It took Lisa a moment to realize what Grandma was talking about. Then she said, 'Alice tells tales.'

'About you?'

'Mostly about me. She told Laurent I'd said I didn't want a French stepfather.'

'Was it true? Had you said that?'

'Only after they'd said a lot of things about us. Pierre said English ladies couldn't be proper mothers because they liked dogs better than children.'

'And I suppose you said French people ate frogs and snails?'

'Yes. And horses.'

'I expect we've all done that,' Grandma said.

'I haven't!' Lisa said, outraged.

'You wouldn't have known. Anyway . . . You said their father makes them behave properly to your mother?'

'Ye-es.'

'They don't say that sort of thing to her? Do they do what she tells them?'

'Generally they do. Sometimes they pretend not to understand. But it's stupid. They know English perfectly well.'

'So what does Fanny . . . your mother . . . do about that?'

[6]

'Says it in French. The first time, it was funny. They didn't expect her to be able to.'

'Your mother speaks French very well. She lived in France for more than a year.'

'That's another thing. They say her accent is not Parisian, whatever that means.'

'Say so to her?'

'No. To me.'

'Stupid kids,' Grandma said, and Lisa was encouraged to go on with the story. 'So we had a fight.'

'Do you fight a lot?'

'Quite a lot,' Lisa said, and thought it was peculiar that if Grandpa had asked this question, she would have answered differently. Grandpa would not like the idea that she and those French kids fought, but Grandma, she somehow knew, did not mind. She might even be quite pleased to think that Lisa would have won.

3

Thinking about Pierre and Alice had made Lisa forget about ghosts, but later that day she remembered. She had a feeling that when her grandmother had said she wasn't sure if she'd seen a ghost or not, that was almost as good as admitting that she had.

'You did see a ghost once, then, Grandma?'

Her grandmother said, 'Oh, Lisa! You do go on, don't you?'

'I just want to know. Did you?'

'I don't know. He could have been just an ordinary boy who happened to be in the house.'

'What house?'

'In John's house. In London.'

'Did he just suddenly appear out of nowhere?'

'No, he didn't. And he wasn't carrying his head under his arm, either.'

'Weren't you frightened, though? Was it dark?'

'It wasn't dark at all. It was the middle of the afternoon.'

Lisa was surprised. She hadn't thought of ghosts appearing in daylight.

'Why did you think he was a ghost?' she asked.

'I didn't, not then.'

'But you did think afterwards that perhaps he was a ghost?'

'It was what he said. John . . . Grandpa . . . thought that an ordinary boy wouldn't have known so much.'

'What did he say?' This was getting interesting.

'Lisa, I really don't want to talk about it.'

'But Grandma . . .'

'Come and help me tie up the little trees. Here! You carry this.' 'This' was a bowl of corks, each with a hole at one end.

'How can you tie up trees? Tie them what to?' Lisa asked.

'You'll see.'

In the garden shed Lisa's grandma collected canes and twine and secateurs and they walked down over the lawn, where Grandpa was at his endless job of rooting out dandelions, to a row of little cypress trees, which were now just tall enough to need support for their feathery heads. Lisa's grandma thrust a cane into the ground next to the first baby tree and tied its soft upper stem to the stick. 'There, little tree! Now you won't bend over and break if it snows,' she said. She put a cork on the top of the cane. 'So that I don't get that sharp top in my eye when I'm looking to see that it's all right,' she said.

It was quite a long row of little trees, and by the time each one had been tied up, Lisa was tired of standing still. She went into the vegetable garden and found half a handful of tiny wild strawberries. She picked a bean pod and shelled out five small pink beans, which tasted sweet and surprised to be caught so young. She contemplated the plum trees; it had not been a good plum year, her grandma said. Last year they had had more plums than they knew what to do with; this year there would not be enough for a single pie. There were plenty of apples, but they were still small and green and Lisa could feel, without tasting one, the acid dryness that it would bring to her mouth. She went back to the lawn. Grandpa was there, digging up the tough roots with a long forked tool. When she got near, Lisa could hear him singing softly to himself under his breath. He saw her bare legs above red canvas shoes coming to a halt beside him, and he looked up.

'Have you finished with the tree babies?' he asked.

'Mm. Grandma's gone back to the house.'

[9]

He looked at his watch. 'Another five minutes and I shall stop and come in for some tea.'

Lisa remembered that she had a question she wanted answered, and that she must ask it when her grandma wasn't there. Best to take Grandpa by surprise. She said, 'What did the little boy ghost talk to you about, Grandpa?'

He stopped pushing the forked tool down beside the bold yellow face of the dandelion and said, 'What little boy ghost?'

'Grandma said . . . She sort of told me about him. She said he might have been a real boy and not a ghost at all. But he was, wasn't he? She said he was in the house you lived in. In London.'

One of her grandfather's habits that Lisa liked best was his slow way of doing things. He spoke slowly, he moved slowly about the house and the garden – though he could walk very fast when he chose to. And he generally took time to answer questions, which showed that, unlike most grown-up people, he really considered what you had asked.

He took a longish time now, before he said, 'I think it was not a real boy.'

'Because he disappeared? Did he disappear suddenly?'

'No. Not because of disappearing. Because of what he said.'

'What did he say, Grandpa?'

'He said what a real boy of that time would not have been able to tell. He could not have known.'

'What was it?' Lisa asked.

'I am not going to tell you all that he said. He told me of things that had not happened yet. Bad things. Terrible things. Things I would never have dreamed of.'

'Are they going to happen now? Soon?'

'They happened a long time ago. Before you were born. Hopefully they will never happen again.'

Lisa was relieved, but at the same time disappointed. She didn't exactly want terrible things to happen, but the idea of them was exciting as well as frightening.

'So the boy was right. He did know,' she said.

'He was right.'

'When did you see him? Grandma said in your house in London. I thought you and Grandma had always lived here.'

'We have lived here for more than thirty years, but we both lived in London when we were children.'

'You mean, you saw the ghost when you were quite little? Weren't you frightened?'

'You have forgotten. I didn't know then that he was a ghost.'

'But you would have been frightened if you'd known?'

'Probably not as frightened as I would be now.'

'But you're grown up!' Lisa exclaimed.

'I suppose you think children are the only ones to get frightened. I can tell you, grown-up people can be terribly frightened too.'

'Of ghosts?'

'Of worse than ghosts. Frightened of other men and women. Their neighbours. Their friends, even, and that is worst of all.'

'How could they be frightened of their friends?'

'People who have been friends and who have changed.'

'That's horrible! I wouldn't have friends who did that.'

'There can be difficult choices,' Grandpa said. He pushed the fork further down and pulled up the dandelion. It had a long straggly root. 'Poor flower. Although I know it is necessary, I don't like destroying something like this that has worked so hard to get its living,' he said.

Lisa wasn't interested in dandelions. She wanted to hear more about the ghost. 'Did you say anything to the ghost boy?' she asked.

'I think I asked him who he was. I didn't remember seeing him before.'

'And then he told you the terrible thing that was going to happen?'

[11]

'Not quite like that. It was difficult for me to understand. My English wasn't so good, and he was speaking quickly and in a way I was not used to.'

'What did he say?'

Grandpa got up from his knees slowly. 'Ugh, how old I am! To stand up after I have been kneeling tells me that all my muscles and my joints are a hundred years old.'

'You're not nearly a hundred, Grandpa! Grandma told me, you're only sixty something.'

'When I have been weeding, I am a hundred. But when I wake up on a sunny morning and Evelyn brings me good coffee and a hot roll in bed, I am twenty-five. You will discover this, Lisa. No one is all of one age after he has finished with being a baby.'

They walked back towards the house. Lisa didn't want to leave the subject of the ghost boy. She asked, 'Are you frightened of anything now, Grandpa?'

As usual, he thought before he answered, 'Yes, sometimes. But now I am frightened of different things from when I was younger. I am not frightened now of people so much. More of what no one can avoid. I am frightened of being ill for many years before I die. Of being a nuisance to your grandmother. Of being boring. Just now you and I should be frightened that we don't have time to wash our hands clean before we go in to tea.'

Lisa recognized that this was the end of the conversation. They washed their hands and went into the kitchen for tea. Lisa did not listen to her grandparents' conversation. She went on thinking about the ghost boy, and wondering about the terrible things that he had told Grandpa. She had a feeling that there would never be a time when her grandfather would be ready to tell her what they were.

4

That night, on the way up to her bath, she tried again. This time she would approach the subject cautiously, by round-about means.

'You and Grandpa knew each other when you were children, didn't you?'

'You know we did. Lisa, when you're out of the bath, please remember to give it a rub round.'

'Did you think then that you'd marry each other?'

'Of course not. We never thought we'd see each other after we grew up.'

'Why not? Didn't you like each other?'

'We got on all right. But no one could have known that he'd spend the rest of his life in England.'

'But you were in England. Weren't you?'

'Lisa, you know quite well that Grandpa wasn't English. He was born in Austria. He didn't come to this country until he was six.'

'Why did he come here then?'

'Because his father got a job in London, so the whole family came and they stayed for five years. That was when we got to know each other. Mr Rosen rented a house op-posite ours, so John and I met in the Square garden.'

'Why do you say the square garden? You mean it wasn't round?'

'Nothing to do with its shape. It was the garden that belonged to the Square where we both lived.'

'Was it in your house that you saw the ghost? Or in his?'

Lisa's grandma took no notice of this remark. 'Lisa, you're

talking too much. Go and get into that bath quickly or the water will be cold.'

'Won't you come and talk to me while I'm in the bath?'

'No, I will not! You think I've got nothing better to do? I've got all the vegetables to prepare before supper.'

As soon as she was dry and dressed in pyjamas and dressing gown, Lisa went down to the kitchen. She wasn't going to drop the subject.

She found her grandmother scrubbing potatoes and pricking them with a fork.

'Baked potatoes? Wonderful! They're my favourite. Except for chips.'

'Much better for you than chips,' Lisa's grandmother said. She dried the potatoes and put them into the microwave.

'Grandma, what were the terrible things that the boy ghost told Grandpa?'

'Who said anything about terrible things?'

'Grandpa did. And he said that afterwards they did happen, so that was why he thought the boy was a ghost, not real, or he wouldn't have known so much.'

'They were happening then. It wouldn't have been impossible for the boy to have known about them, even if we didn't.'

'What sort of things?' Lisa asked.

'Things that were going on in Germany when Hitler was in power. And I'm not going to tell you any more. It's all over now, thank goodness. Would you lay the table, please, Lisa? Knives and forks and spoons and don't forget the pepper and salt.'

While she was putting the cutlery on the table, Lisa considered her next question. 'Was it what the ghost boy said that made Grandpa decide not to go back to Germany?'

'Austria. No, the whole family went back when Mr Rosen's job in London came to an end.'

'Who was the whole family? I didn't know Grandpa had brothers and sisters.'

[14]

'He didn't have any brothers. There was just him and one sister, quite a bit younger.'

'Where is she now? I didn't know he had a sister.'

'She died. A long time ago.'

'Was it after the war that Grandpa came back to England and you met him again?'

'No, he was here again before the war started. He'd meant just to stay for the Easter holidays, but then it wasn't safe for him to go back, so he stayed on.'

'Why wasn't it safe?'

'Don't you know anything about the last war?' Lisa's grandma asked.

Lisa didn't know much. 'We were fighting Germany, weren't we?'

'We were fighting Hitler, and the countries he'd taken over. Germany and Austria. Italy was in it with him, too.'

'If Grandpa had gone back before the war, then, he'd have been fighting us in the war? He'd have been the enemy?'

'He wouldn't have been fighting. He wasn't old enough.'

'Did his father fight us?'

'No.'

'What happened to his father, then?'

'He died during the war. Lisa, I really don't want to talk about it. Would you get the water out of the fridge, please? And then you can go to Grandpa's study and tell him supper's ready.'

It was the end of the conversation. Over supper they talked about the garden and what needed doing in it the next day if it didn't rain. But Lisa wasn't satisfied. She knew that some people didn't like to admit that they might believe in ghosts, and thought that children shouldn't hear about such things. She felt that as well as not wanting to talk about the little boy ghost they might have seen, her grandparents were reluctant to talk about Grandpa's family. There was some mystery about them which she wasn't to know.

After she'd gone to bed that night, Lisa searched her memory of stories she'd read and television programmes she had seen for the sort of shameful secret which a respectable family would want to hide. Could Grandpa's father have been a spy? He had lived in England and in Germany, or Austria, whichever it was, so he could have been employed as a secret agent. Or had he traded in illegal drugs? Perhaps he had cheated at cards, or refused to fight a duel, so that everyone had called him a coward. People didn't fight duels nowadays, but they might have done when Grandpa's father was young. It was exciting to think that there was a family secret, and Lisa wasn't going to give up trying to discover what it was. She'd hardly made this resolution when she found herself getting confused, and she fell asleep before she had invented any more likely explanation of the mystery.

Two days later, her mother came to fetch her home. Lisa was running to hug her when she saw two more figures getting out of the car, and she stopped. She saw her grandmother and mother kiss each other, and then the introductions. She was too far off to hear, but she knew that her mother was saying, 'This is Alice, and this is Pierre, Mum.' She saw the smiles and handshakes, and she thought, 'That's right. All polite and goody now, so Grandma will think how nice they are and that I'm stupid not to like them.' She wasn't going to be any part of it. She stepped back into the little spinney where she would be hidden by the tall grass. She heard her mother say, 'Where's Lisa?' and then her grandma called her: 'Lisa! Lisa! Your mother's here!' But she stayed where she was. She didn't mean to join the others a minute sooner than she had to. From behind the trunks of the young trees, she watched them all go into the house.

Presently different voices were calling her name. Pierre and Alice had been sent out to find her. It was maddening that they seemed to know where to look. They came directly to the corner of the garden, where she hadn't a hope of hiding unless she climbed into the yew tree or lay down flat in the grass. That would be too much like playing a game with them. She wouldn't pay them that much of a compliment. It would be treating them as equals. So when they came up to her, she was leaning against the smooth trunk of the balsam poplar, sniffing one of its resinous leaves.

'*La voilà!*' Pierre said.

'*La grandmère te cherche,*' Alice said. She spoke insultingly slowly and clearly, as if to an idiot or a very small child.

'*Elle nous a ordonné de te trouver,*' Pierre said.

'Say it in English. I know you can,' Lisa said.

'Your . . . grandmother . . . sent us to . . . discover you,' Pierre said.

'She wants you . . . to come at the house. She said this . . . behaving is not . . . polite,' Alice said.

'She didn't!'

'No? You have heard?'

'She wouldn't say that to you. She didn't, did she?' Lisa asked Pierre, who was standing there, silent.

When she had first heard about Laurent's two children, Lisa had felt a sort of interest in Pierre, had even thought she might quite like him. But that was before she'd known that he and Alice were to come to live with them. Once they were established in the house in London, she disliked him only a little less than she disliked Alice. Although he spoke English a great deal better than his sister, he seldom talked to Lisa, leaving Alice to make all the necessary communications. It wasn't because he didn't care to talk. Lisa had heard him and Alice chattering volubly to each other, in French, of course, and he talked, too, to Fanny. Lisa felt that he didn't think her worth his notice. He despised her. Very well, then she would despise him.

'*Il faut se mettre à table,*' Alice said.

'English!' Lisa spat at her.

'We have to sit at the table. Your grandmother has . . .

made the *déjeuner*. She says to hurry that it does not get cold,' Alice said, and turned back towards the house, followed by Pierre and, a long way behind and very cross, by Lisa.

Lisa had been looking forward to the drive back to London that afternoon. She wanted to tell her mother what she'd done while she'd been away, to grumble about Grandma's strict rules about watching television and washing up. More than anything, she wanted to find out if her mother knew anything about the ghost boy. But all this was impossible, with Alice and Pierre sitting in the back seat of the car and listening to everything she said. She answered her mother's questions as shortly as she could, and for most of the journey there was silence in front, and behind a whispered conversation in French.

Lisa knew she was behaving badly. When she was in bed that evening, she was not surprised that her mother, shutting the bedroom door behind her, came straight to the point.

'Lisa. What's the matter? Why are you being like this?'

'I'm not being like anything.'

'Yes, you are. You're being sulky and rude. Weren't you happy with John and Evelyn?'

'Yes, I was.'

'My mother said you'd seemed quite all right. In fact they both said how helpful you'd been and that they'd enjoyed having you. So what's wrong now?'

Lisa didn't answer.

'Is it Pierre and Alice?'

'Why did you bring them to fetch me? I wanted it to be just you.'

'I brought them because they're part of the family and we all do things together.'

'Not my family they're not,' Lisa said.

Her mother sat on the side of the bed. 'Look, love. Pierre and Alice are Laurent's family and you are mine, and now that Laurent and I are married we're all one family. I know

[18]

it isn't easy, suddenly having a ready-made brother and sister to share with, after you've been the only one. But you have to get used to it. This is how it's going to be, and you'll be the one who gets hurt if you kick against it all the time.'

There was no possible way of denying this. Lisa said, 'They don't like it either.'

'I don't expect they do. It's worse for them, having to come and live in a country they don't know.'

'They could have stayed with their mother,' Lisa said.

'That's another thing. She doesn't really want them. You might be sorry for them. I know you haven't had a father that you can remember, but at least he didn't choose to die and leave us. It can't be much fun discovering that your mother would rather not have you with her. You must see that.'

Lisa did, but she wasn't ready to be sorry for Pierre and Alice. 'They've got their father.'

'But they wouldn't have if they'd stayed in France, would they? I'd feel terrible if I thought they'd been separated from him because of me.'

'I wish you hadn't married him,' Lisa said. She'd never said it out loud before.

'I expect you do. I know it's difficult for you. All I can do is hope you'll come to like Laurent's kids more than you do now. And if there's anything I can do to make it easier, you must tell me.'

'There isn't anything.' There was no point in saying, 'Send them back to France.'

'All right. Just remember, you can always talk to me if things get bad. Now, go to sleep, love. Whatever happens, you're my dearest girl.'

5

The next day, Lisa was standing in front of the long mirror in the hall, trying to judge how she looked in the dress Grandma had given her. It was the prettiest dress she'd ever had, dark green and silky, with little ruffles round the neck and cuffs. She had turned away from the mirror and was peering over her left shoulder, trying to see how the dress looked at the back, when she heard Pierre's voice from a step or two above her. He and Alice were both there. They must have crept down, mouse quiet, to spy on her.

'*Fais attention quand tu te regards dans un miroir,*' Pierre said.

'Talk English!' Lisa snapped.

'*C'est dommage que tu ne comprends pas la langue française.*'

'English, or I won't talk to you.'

'I would not be unhappy if you did not talk. I said, be careful how you look in mirrors. They are dangerous, didn't you know?'

'That's stupid! How can mirrors be dangerous?'

'*Les miroirs sont les portes par lesquelles la mort va et vient,*' Pierre said.

'I don't understand.'

'A great man wrote it. You will never have heard of him.' And indeed the name he said meant nothing to Lisa.

'What does it mean, then?'

'He is saying that mirrors are the doors for Death to enter. And to . . . to go away.'

'It is stupid! How could . . . Death come through a mirror? Mirrors aren't doors.'

'Perhaps they are doors for *la mort*. That is, Death.'

'I'm not frightened of death,' Lisa said, not quite truthfully.

'Then you are *stupide*. Very, very *stupide*. Everyone is frightened of death.'

'Shut up!'

Pierre made a face. 'You are most impolite. You are . . . a rude child.'

'Don't call me a child! You're not that much older than me!'

'It is true, you are old enough to have learned how to behave with *politesse*.'

'It's you that don't know how to behave. I expect it's because you're French.' Lisa's voice made this last remark an insult.

'I am pleased to be French. I do not want ever to be *anglais* . . . English,' Alice said.

'That's good, because you never will be, however hard you try.'

'I will not try. The English people are cold . . . and some of them are rude and ugly,' Alice said.

'I suppose you think French people are polite because they shake hands and kiss each other all the time. I think it looks silly.'

'You were never in France. How do you know what French people do?'

From the stairs, Pierre said, coolly, 'This is stupid talk. Leave her, Alice. Then she can look in the *miroir* and think she is pretty.'

'Her nose is not pretty,' Alice said.

'Leave her nose. It is an English nose. Probably English girls like to have such noses.'

He sounded horribly superior. Lisa couldn't bear it. She shot an arm between the banisters and grabbed at his leg. He stepped back, missed his footing and fell down the three steps to the hall floor. He didn't get up at once, but lay there groaning. She approached him cautiously. She couldn't see his face. The groans told her that he wasn't unconscious, but he might have broken something, in which case she'd have to go for help. She came closer. An arm shot out and caught her ankle. She pulled away, almost got clear, then he caught her again, this time by the other ankle and her skirt. He'd been shamming hurt, he was laughing now, not groaning, and as she strained to get free, she heard the sound of tearing silk. Pierre heard it too and let go so suddenly that Lisa staggered backwards, nearly fell, and hit her head against the corner of the wooden pillar at the bottom of the stairs. The corner was sharp and the pain was intense. She was mad with fury. She kicked Pierre as viciously as she knew how, and was pleased to see him double up, clutching himself, this time really hurt.

The noise brought Lisa's mother from the kitchen.

'What's the matter? Pierre, what's happened to you?' But he didn't answer.

'He fell down the stairs,' Lisa said.

'How far? From the top? Pierre, try to tell me where it hurts.'

'Only three steps. He can't be hurt badly,' Lisa said.

'Did you fall too, Lisa? Look at your new dress!'

'He caught hold of me and wouldn't let me go,' Lisa said.

'You were quarrelling again. I've told you, I won't have it. You've got to learn to live together,' Fanny said.

'She hurt him,' Alice said.

'Did you, Lisa?'

'I hit my head against that,' Lisa said, pointing to the wooden post.

Pierre got up off the floor. He looked pale, and Lisa felt a moment's compunction. It didn't last. Now he would tell her mother how she'd kicked him.

'You sure you haven't broken anything?' Fanny asked.

'I have not broken anything,' Pierre said.

'You didn't hit your head too?'

'No.'

[22]

'What about you, Lisa? Was it very hard? You don't feel giddy? Have you got a headache?'

Lisa said, 'No.' She was still waiting for Pierre to tell on her.

'Do you, Pierre? *As-tu mal à la tête?*'

'*Non.*' He didn't say anything else.

'You don't look quite right to me. You'd better go and sit down somewhere quietly. Or lie on your bed. Lisa, go and take off that dress and bring it down so that I can see if it's just pulled out at the seam or if the silk is torn. Why you should want to fight when you're wearing a brand new dress is something I don't understand. And as I said, I won't have you fighting. You're both of you too old to squabble like babies.'

She went back to the kitchen. Pierre went upstairs without another word. Alice went too, and Lisa heard her follow her brother into his room.

At least he hadn't given her away. He hadn't said that she had started the fight, nor that she had kicked him. Lisa was frightened as the result of that kick. She began to feel a little sorry for him, but much sorrier for herself when she discovered that the silk skirt had indeed torn from the waist almost down to the hem. It would never be the same again. Mum was going to be really cross, and Lisa did not look forward to having to explain the damage to her grandmother. She changed back into jeans and a shirt as slowly as she could, putting off the bad moment when she'd have to show Fanny the ruined dress.

She went slowly down the stairs, too. It was lucky that her mother was intent on her sketches which were spread over the kitchen table, so that all she said was, 'Is that your dress? Put it over the back of that chair, will you? I'll look at it when I've finished this.' Lisa didn't wait to ask what 'this' was. She escaped out of the door and upstairs to her own room, leaving her mother scratching energetically at a drawing, with sheets of paper covered by half-finished sketches all round her. Lisa hoped that 'this' would take a long time, so that when her mother came to examine the torn silk, she'd no longer be feeling cross about the quarrel.

She lay on her bed and read Rumer Godden's *A Dolls' House*. She'd read it before and she knew it wasn't the sort of book a girl of eleven should want to read again, but she didn't feel like tackling anything more difficult. In spite of what she'd told her mother, her head did ache and she was unusually tired. Presently the print began to jump about and she couldn't be bothered to keep her eyes open. She let the book fall out of her hand and slid, deliciously, into sleep.

She was woken by her mother, who was standing just inside the door.

'Lisa? I want to speak to you.'

Lisa said, 'Mm,' drugged by sleep at an unaccustomed time.

'Have you been asleep? All right, come along to my room when you're properly awake. In five minutes.' She was gone.

Lisa stretched and yawned. She was cold. That was odd, it had been a hot September afternoon, and the sun was shining directly into her room. She was astonished to see by her bedside clock that it was nearly seven o'clock. She'd been asleep for more than two hours. She got off the bed and found an old pullover to put on over her shirt. She wasn't going to change for supper. No doubt Alice would be there, with newly-brushed hair shining, neat and pretty from head to foot. Lisa wasn't going to try to be anything like that.

Fanny's room looked out east into the garden and now it was dim and shadowy. Fanny, however, was not there. Lisa hesitated in the doorway, then her eye caught a square of pale light which, surprisingly, was on a wall which had no windows. It was the reflection of the window opposite, in the mirror which hung directly over her mother's dressing table. She was intrigued, not for the first time, by the fact that in a mirror you could see things sideways on, which, if

[24]

you stood directly in front of it, didn't appear at all. Mirrors were certainly mysterious, but – dangerous? What nonsense! Lisa had known this mirror all her life. You could say she had seen herself grow up in it. It was not English. It had belonged to Grandpa's family; he had known it as long as he could remember. The heavy frame was of dark carved wood, made more than a hundred years ago, Lisa knew. It had hung in the sitting room of his parents' apartment, Grandpa said, in . . . somewhere in Austria. Lisa couldn't remember the name of the place. The picture reflected in its shining glass was very clear and distinct, except in one of the lower corners, where there was a star fracture like a spider's web, with long thin cracks radiating out from the central black hole.

'What happened? Who broke it?' Lisa had asked her mother.

'No idea. My father says it wasn't like that when he was a little boy. When he went back to Austria after the war, he found that the mirror was the only thing left in his father's apartment. Everything else had been taken away.'

'Why? Did his mother and father move somewhere else?'

'They'd left a long time before.'

'Why did the people who took the other things, leave the mirror, then?'

'Grandpa told me that they probably thought it was unlucky because of that crack.'

'Did he bring it back to England then?'

'That's right. He gave it to me because my mother said she didn't like it. She says the frame is too heavy.'

'What did Grandpa go back to Austria for?'

'He went back to Vienna to see if any of his family were still alive after the war.'

'Grandma told me they'd all died.'

'He thought there was just a chance one of them might have escaped. He thought he might find that his sister was still alive.'

[25]

'I somehow thought she'd died when she was a baby.'

'No. She'd have been nine or ten when . . .'

'When what?'

'When they all died.'

'Did they all die together?'

'Probably. I don't know.'

'Doesn't Grandpa know?'

'I don't think so, but anyway, don't ask him about it. I know he feels bad about being the only one of the family who survived.'

There was some mystery that Fanny wasn't going to explain. Lisa considered everything she knew about the war, which was very little. She knew that England and Germany had fought each other and that there'd been bombs in London. She supposed that the English air force had dropped bombs on Germany too. Perhaps it had been an English bomb that had killed Grandpa's mother and father and his sister. That would explain why he wouldn't want to talk about it. Now that he was English himself, he might feel almost as if he'd helped to kill his own family.

Standing in front of the mirror now, Lisa wondered what it had seen in the more than a hundred years since it had been made. It was much the grandest mirror in the house and she had usually liked the picture of herself that she saw in it. She didn't much like that picture now. In these old clothes and with hair that stood up spikily all over her head just as it had done when she'd woken, she was undeniably plain. Not pretty, like Aleese. She made a face at herself. She turned her head so as to try to see if her profile was any more interesting than her full face, and what Pierre had meant when he had said she had an English nose. She hadn't realized before that it is impossible to see your profile properly unless you have two mirrors. Lisa picked up Fanny's little oval hand mirror, and tried to look at two reflections at once. It took a little time to get the two mirrors, the one on the wall and the other in her hand, to reflect each

[26]

other, so that she could get a sideways look at herself. It was surprisingly difficult. She kept on getting bits of the room behind her without Lisa; or Lisa frontways on, which she'd seen hundreds of times before and wasn't at the moment interested in. And then she got it. It was best, she found, to stand with her back to the large mirror and to look directly into the hand mirror tilted so that it reflected her image in the other mirror. No, her profile wasn't any more beautiful than her full face; but she didn't think her nose was much worse than most people's. It wasn't a great proboscis, like poor Mary Ponders' at school.

Out of the corner of her eye, she saw something move, and was confused. How had she seen it? In a reflection in a mirror? Or out there in the room beyond? She turned to look. But the room was empty, cool and growing darker as the sky beyond the windows gradually lost light. Lisa turned back to look in the two mirrors. Again, out of the corner of her eye, she caught a movement, a quivering, a flicker of light. Were the curtains moving? But there was no wind, and when she looked at them directly they were still. She looked into the big mirror and saw only her own face, pale against the twilight background. Then she looked into the hand mirror, and there, in the reflection of the big mirror she saw the back of her own head, and behind it, not the familiar outlines of the windows, the curtains and the end of her mother's bed, but darkness, in which there was the flicker of candles. She saw, too, what looked like heads, the bowed heads of a number of people. She could almost imagine that she could hear a sort of mumble, an intoning, a chant.

But that was stupid. How could she see something reflected in a mirror which wasn't there when she looked at the real room in front of her? How could she have thought she heard voices in that cool, sane silence? Lisa almost threw down the hand mirror and ran out of the room.

6

She was sitting on the side of her bed, still shaking, when there was a tap on the door and her mother came in.

'Lisa, I'm sorry I wasn't . . . What's the matter?'

'Nothing.'

Fanny shut the door behind her. Not a good sign.

'I'm very cross with you.'

'I'm sorry about the dress, Mum. Pierre had got hold of me and I was trying to get away . . .'

'The dress is bad enough. I don't know if I'll be able to mend it so that it doesn't show too much. It isn't that. It's the way you're behaving to Pierre. You kicked him.'

So he had told, after all. 'I kicked him because he made me hit my head on the banister post.'

'Wasn't that after you'd made him fall down stairs?'

'He only fell down three steps. He wasn't hurt at all. He was shamming.'

'You hurt him a lot when you kicked him. Lisa, I said, I will not have you fighting. I don't say that you've got to like Pierre and Alice now, though I hope you will later on. But you have got to behave politely. They are your guests.'

'You said we were all one family. You don't have guests in a family.'

'Never mind what I said. I'm telling you now, that I expect you to keep the peace and not to start fights. Pierre wouldn't have done anything to you, if you hadn't begun it.'

'He's a sneak. I suppose he came whining to you and said I started it.'

'He didn't tell me anything.'

'Alice did, then.'

'Alice didn't tell me anything until I asked her.'

'She didn't have to tell you then. I suppose she said it was all my fault.'

Fanny didn't answer that. Lisa knew that she'd guessed right. She added another black mark against Alice in her mind. She said, 'I suppose it's because they're French that they have to tell tales.' She was not surprised that this made her mother really angry.

'I think you'd better stay up here for the rest of the evening. You needn't come down again. I'll bring you up some supper.'

'I'm not going to be sent to bed as if I was a baby!' Lisa cried out.

'You can come down and join the rest of the family when you've learned to behave as if you weren't a baby. I don't want to see you again till you're ready to do that,' Lisa's mother said, and left her.

Lisa was too angry even to cry. She hadn't had a row like this with her mother since she was tiny. She couldn't remember when she'd seen Mum as furious, or when she'd been so wild herself. Of course they'd quarrelled, mothers and daughters always did, she knew that from her friends. But those quarrels had been about clothes and hair and watching telly and bedtime; tame, ordinary affairs compared with this. Lisa had frequently said, as all children do, 'It isn't fair!' She had never before felt pushed out. Fanny had never said, 'I don't want to see you . . .' Lisa had been the person she'd wanted to see more than anyone else in the world. Now she could afford to do without her. Now she'd got not only Laurent, but also two new children. They were her new family. She was being horrible to Lisa because of Pierre and Alice. Perhaps she already preferred them to her own daughter. Of course, they knew how to behave, especially in front of her. Horrible Alice didn't trip people up and tear her nice new clothes; she remained pretty and smiling and smug. And sneaky. And revolting and stinking and French. Worse than Pierre, because at least he hadn't told on her.

She opened her bedroom door and listened. She could hear the radio programme to which her mother usually finished cooking the supper. From the sitting room, she heard, faintly, the sound of the television. It stopped abruptly and a door opened. She heard Laurent saying something in French, then footsteps went along the hall towards the kitchen. The smell of something good floated up the stairs as the kitchen door was opened. But Lisa wasn't hungry. She heard her mother's voice among the others before the kitchen door was shut again. The radio was switched off and she could just catch the murmur of conversation as Fanny, presumably, put the supper on the table. She must have forgotten that she'd said she'd bring Lisa's meal up to her. That was the last straw. Lisa shut the door again. Her tears were tears of rage as much as of misery.

Almost at once the door was opened by Laurent, holding a tray which he put down on the bedside table.

'Your supper,' he said.

'Mum said she was going to bring it up.'

'She is tired. She has been working hard and then she was upset by you and Pierre.'

There seemed nothing to say to this.

'Have you anything to say to your mother? A message?'

Lisa shook her head.

'Not a word of thank you?'

Silence.

'I don't know if I should say, "Enjoy your meal." '

'I'm not going to eat it. I'm not hungry.'

'Shall I take it away?'

She nodded.

'You are sure?'

'I said so, didn't I?'

He picked up the tray and left without another word. Lisa was pleased that she'd refused it. That would show

Mum that she wasn't a baby, to be calmed down by being fed. She hoped that Laurent hadn't noticed that she'd been crying. But he almost certainly had, he was a noticing sort of person. In her present mood, she would have liked to feel that she hated him almost as much as his children, but she hadn't the energy to feel that strongly about him. Before he'd brought those two to live here, she had thought him quite tolerable. He had treated her with a distant friendliness, and had talked to her seriously, as if she had been nearly grown-up. If he hadn't married her mother, she could have liked him a lot. Of course she'd been jealous of him. After living alone with Fanny for as long as she could remember, it hadn't been easy to accept that this strange man was going to become part of their household, with a claim to Fanny's time and love. But Fanny had taken the trouble to talk about it. She had said, 'I can't expect you to feel about Laurent as if he were your real father. You'll probably find it difficult when he comes to live here, when it's been just you and me for so long. Having a third person here isn't going to be easy, I do know that. I'll try to be understanding, and I want you to remember that you are always my darling girl. Nothing changes that, or makes any difference to how much I love you.'

'Oh yes. Look how much you're loving me now!' Lisa thought. 'And when you told me about Laurent, you never said anything about his stinking kids. You didn't tell me then that they were coming here to live with us and to muck up my life and make me miserable. It was all going to be wonderful, I was going to have a proper father at last and we were going to be a real family. I didn't want a stepfather much, and I certainly didn't want a stepbrother and sister. Especially horrible French kids like they are.'

7

At breakfast the next morning, there was plenty of conversation round the kitchen table, but Lisa did not join in. She gathered that Laurent was taking Alice and Pierre to visit the school they would be attending when term began the next week. Fanny asked Lisa, 'What are you going to do? I've got this job I must finish, so I'm afraid I'll be working for most of the day.'

'I'll be all right,' Lisa said.

'Have you written yet to my mother and father to thank them for having you to stay? You'd better do that today, then.'

'I said "Thank you" when I left,' Lisa said.

'It's polite to write as well.' At the word 'polite' Lisa saw Pierre look at her. His expression said: 'You wouldn't know what is polite and what isn't. You are a rude child.'

She hated him.

'You'd better get ready to go out, you two. You've got to be at the Lycée by eleven, so you haven't got a lot of time,' Fanny said to Pierre and Alice. To Laurent, she said, 'Yes, you go too. Lisa can help me clear away the breakfast things.'

That was an excuse, Lisa was sure, to have her alone to scold. She could avoid this by offering to clear away and wash up by herself. If her mother really had a rush job on, she'd probably accept and be grateful; but then wouldn't it look as if Lisa was trying to get back into favour? Or as if she was apologizing for yesterday's fight? So she stacked plates and carried them to the sink and dried what her mother washed without speaking. Fanny didn't speak either until they had finished. Then she put an arm round Lisa's unwelcoming shoulders and said, 'Let's forget yesterday. We'll pretend it never happened. I know it isn't easy, having Pierre and Alice living here. I don't always like it particularly myself.'

'Don't you?' Lisa said, astonished.

'Suddenly having three kids instead of one? Sometimes I think it could be fun. I was always sorry you were an only, I'd have loved to have had another. Other times I get fed up. But it isn't as difficult for me as it is for you, because I happen quite to like them. I think Pierre has an interesting mind. He's got a lot of imagination and a sort of intellectual curiosity, like his father. But that doesn't mean I don't understand how you're feeling.'

Lisa's throat went lumpy, though there didn't seem any reason why she should suddenly be near tears. She managed to say, 'I'm sorry.' Fanny tightened the arm, kissed her on the back of the neck, and said, 'I must start work. If you're feeling very kind, would you go round the corner and get me half a pound of butter and a dozen eggs? I'm obviously not used to catering for such a large family. I'm always running out of something. You can take the money out of my purse. It's there on the dresser.'

It was a quiet morning. Lisa did the shopping and finished, rather ashamed of herself, reading *A Doll's House*, because although she knew how it ended there was a satisfaction in reading it in Rumer Godden's own words. Also, she was putting off the business of writing the Thank-you letter. The first sentence, Thank-you-for-having-me-I-enjoyed-it-very-much, was easy, but after that she was stuck. She hadn't done anything interesting since she'd come home. She wasn't going to tell Grandma about the fight with Pierre, or how the new dress had got torn. If Grandma had been the only person to read this letter she might have let herself write what she really felt about Pierre and Alice; but she knew that Grandpa would read it too, and he wouldn't approve of her complaining about them. He would say that she must try to find out if there wasn't something about them that she liked. Her mother had said that she thought Pierre was interesting. Lisa didn't find him interesting at all, and if he really had a lot of imagination, Lisa hadn't noticed it. Unless he had invented that saying about mirrors being dangerous, just to frighten her.

Perhaps that was the sort of thing her mother had meant. If that was his imagination, it seemed more like stupidity to Lisa. Then she thought of her experience in her mother's room the day before. Was that the sort of danger Pierre had meant? That you could confuse yourself by looking into two mirrors at once, so that you began to see things that weren't really there? At the memory, a tiny shiver ran down Lisa's spine. She was annoyed at herself. She had far too much common sense to begin to be frightened of a couple of mirrors. Some time she would go back to Fanny's room and reassure herself that there was nothing mysterious in the double reflection, nothing to fear.

She wrote, 'Did someone French really say that mirrors are dangerous? Pierre said someone did, but I don't know who it was. It seems silly to me. Probably he's been reading the Looking Glass *Alice*, it's the sort of babyish thing he would do.' She knew this wasn't fair, but she didn't mind. It was most unlikely that Grandma would ever find out if it wasn't true. She wrote, 'They've all gone off this morning to look at the school they're going to next term, P. and A., I mean. Mum is working terribly hard, she's got a rush job doing the pictures for some lousy book. She didn't say it was lousy, but I read it and I thought it was.' This wasn't fair either. It was a book for very young readers, not intended for anyone as old as Lisa. She wrote, 'It's nice being alone in the house with Mum again. I'm sort of looking forward to next term, when I'm starting in my new school, but I'm not sure how much I'll really like it. How many dandelions has Grandpa pulled up now? Can I come and stay with you again next hols? Love, Lisa.'

That was nearly a full page. She'd made her handwriting large on purpose. She went downstairs to look for an envelope and stamps which were kept in one of the drawers of the kitchen dresser, since Fanny had had to give up her workroom for Alice to sleep in.

Her mother looked up from her drawing and said, 'Yes?'

'Sorry to disturb you. I just want an envelope and a stamp for Grandma's letter.'

'You've written? Good girl. You find them, will you?' Fanny said and bent her head over her work again.

When she'd posted her letter, Lisa made two mugs of tea and silently put one beside her deeply concentrating mother. She took the other upstairs and on the way to her own room was reminded of what had happened – or, rather of what she was sure hadn't happened – the evening before. Sitting in bright daylight, drinking tea out of a solid china mug, she felt sure that she'd made some stupid mistake yesterday, thinking that she'd seen anything unusual in the big mirror. She felt brave enough to experiment with the two reflections again.

This morning her mother's room was reassuringly normal; the polished wooden bed ends shone in the sun, and shafts of light, alive with dancing particles of dust, slanted in through the windows. Perhaps the movement she'd thought she'd seen yesterday had been one of those whirling eddies. Lisa went to the dressing table and looked into the wall mirror. It reflected only what she would see if she turned her head. The bookcase between two light windows and, through the windows, blue sky, alive with scudding clouds. The end of her mother's bed. A chair with some clothes on it.

She picked up the hand mirror. It was an object she'd always liked, the oval glass set in pale wood, with a thin line of ivory tracing its periphery. It had belonged to Grandpa's mother's mother, which made it at least as old as

[35]

the long mirror. 'Very beautiful she was, my mother told me,' Grandpa had said. He couldn't remember her at all. His mother had had the mirror then, and it should have gone to her daughter. 'Why hadn't it?' Lisa wondered, then remembered that the daughter must have been the little sister who had died.

She looked at herself, first in the long mirror on the wall, then in the delicate little mirror in her hand. Both showed the same Lisa, with a squarish face, short brown hair, grey eyes and the nose that Pierre had insulted. Now she would try to discover what it could have been that had startled her last night. Again, she turned her back on the large mirror and looked into the small one.

She saw the reflection of the back of her own head. But what was behind it was not her mother's bedroom. This room was high and dark, furnished with a great deal of dark wood, highly polished, and gleaming in the light that came through narrow, casement windows. The walls were hung with pictures, so close together that the walls themselves were invisible. On the shelf of a tall black cabinet were photographs in silver frames, a great many, jostling each other for space. Running from end to end of the table in the centre of the room was a strip of embroidery. A silver vase of pale flowers stood at the exact centre of the runner.

She turned round to face the big mirror. But it reflected only what it should have done, Fanny's sparsely furnished, light bedroom. She turned again and looked into the hand mirror, and saw the dark furniture and the vase of white flowers.

As she looked, she saw the door of the room open. A little girl, came in. She was dark-haired and dark-eyed, and clutched to her chest she was carrying a kitten. She looked round the room and her eyes widened. Lisa knew that she had been seen.

'*Wer bist du*?' the child asked.

Lisa shook her head. She did not understand.

'*Komm*,' the child said. She was beckoning. Her lips moved, and without being able to hear, Lisa knew that she was saying, 'Come here. Come.'

Lisa said, 'How can I?' and heard the words echo as if they had travelled through a long passage. A passage of time.

She could not tell if the girl in the mirror had heard her. She beckoned again. Lisa lifted her eyes and looked out over the hand mirror to her mother's bedroom beyond. 'I'm dreaming, it can't hurt me,' she thought. To the girl, still reflected in the mirror in her hand, she said, 'All right, I'll come,' and moved forward. But when she moved, the mirror in her hand moved too. She said, in relief, 'You see? I can't.' She saw the girl shake her head and point. Lisa knew that now she was saying, 'Not that way. You have to go back.' She thrust out a hand and Lisa felt as if she were being gently propelled backwards towards the big mirror. 'I can't touch it,' she thought, 'Mum's dressing table is in the way.' But instead of feeling the edge of the table against her spine, she stepped easily through what seemed like the arch of a doorway, with the little mirror still in her hand, and now, as she looked, it reflected back to her only her own face. When she looked out over it, she saw, not her mother's pale empty room, but the tall mirror through which she had come. She turned round to face the little girl, who was saying, '*Wie kommst du hierher*?'

Lisa said, 'I don't understand.'

'You are English?' the little girl spoke with a soft, quite pretty accent.

'I'm English, yes. Who are you?'

'How do you come here? This is a private . . . home. Who brought you here?'

'No one brought me. I didn't mean to come here. I don't know where this is.'

It was at this moment that the kitten tried to escape. It

sprang and, as the child tried to catch it, one of its claws caught the flesh of her bare arm and tore a streak of bright blood. Lisa heard the child gasp and heard the soft patter of the kitten's paws as it escaped through the open door. She saw the little girl's face squeeze into a grimace of pain as she opened her mouth to cry. Lisa stepped backwards, away from her, and became aware that she still held the oval mirror in her hand. She turned her back on the scene and looked out over the hand mirror and through the mirror door into her mother's bright, peaceful room. She looked back into the hand mirror and there again was the dark room and the weeping child.

'No!' Lisa said out loud. She put down the mirror, but this time she did not run out of the room. She sat at the dressing table, cold in the sunshine, and tried to believe that what she had seen was only her imagination. There couldn't be anything real about it.

8

She hadn't succeeded when it was time for the midday meal. She and her mother ate it alone; the others hadn't yet returned from the middle of London. When they were eating the fruit which followed soup and bread and cheese, Fanny asked, 'Anything the matter?'

Lisa said, 'I don't think so.'

'What's that supposed to mean?'

'Means I'm not sure.'

'You don't feel ill?'

'No.'

'What then?'

'Can people sometimes see things that aren't really there?'

'You mean like flying saucers?'

'There might really be flying saucers.'

'Like what, then? Do you mean, hallucinations?'

'What are hallucinations?'

'Seeing things that aren't there. Why? I hope you're not having them?'

'I don't think I am. I'm not sure.'

'Tell me,' Fanny said, and stopped eating.

'I thought I saw something in your big mirror, and when I looked properly, it wasn't there.'

'Is that all! I'm always doing that. Yesterday I could have sworn I saw a cat sitting on the bookcase by the sitting room door, and when I looked straight at it, I saw it was the reflection of that Chinese bowl in the glass of the watercolour picture next to it. It looked just like a hunched cat.'

'Did it move?' Lisa asked.

'No. Why? Did what you saw move?'

'I'm not sure. Anyway, you don't think it was real?'

'How can I possibly know if you don't tell me what you saw?'

'It was like a room that wasn't really there.' Now, too late, Lisa found that she didn't want to go on talking about it.

'Perhaps you were half asleep. Dreaming. What were you doing when you thought you saw this?'

'I was looking in a mirror. Two mirrors. I wanted to see what my nose looked like sideways on.'

'I'm not surprised you saw extraordinary things if you were using two mirrors. It's terribly muddling. If you'd ever tried to cut your own hair in a mirror, you'd know that everything works the wrong way round. You think you're getting nearer with the scissors and in fact you're going the other way. Two mirrors makes it more than twice as impossible. Why did you want to see your own nose sideways on?'

'Something Pierre said about it.'

'Uncomplimentary, I suppose. Don't worry, love. It's a very nice nose, whichever way you look at it. How did you manage to use two mirrors?'

'I was using the hand glass as well as the big mirror. So that I could see myself sideways. In the big mirror in the little mirror.' It was muddled, but her mother seemed to understand.

'The reflection of a reflection. I see. It sounds like my imaginary cat.' It would have been comforting to believe this. But her mother's cat hadn't moved, she hadn't found herself talking to a child in a looking glass. She saw her mother looking anxious. She said quickly, 'I expect it was like that. Don't worry, Mum. I'm not going mad or anything.'

It was all very well to reassure her mother. Lisa wished she felt certain herself that there was nothing wrong with her brain. She spent the afternoon doing boring but useful jobs that almost prevented her thinking any more about the scene in the mirrors. She took her new school uniform out of the cupboard and regarded it with a mixture of pride and a sick fear. How would she ever cope with her first term in the big school, where she'd stay till she was nearly grown-up? Sometimes, when she thought about it, she felt sure she'd get on all right, people would like her, she'd do well. Sometimes she saw herself failing horribly, losing the friends she had already, unable to cope with a new standard of work. To reassure herself, she sharpened pencils, rearranged her notebooks, her coloured pens, her folders. She even polished her walking shoes, a job she hated. But getting all her belongings into perfect order didn't seem to do much for her mind. She was still jittery.

She tried reading. She'd found a book belonging to her mother, called *The Diary of Anne Frank*, and someone, she couldn't remember who, had said that it was something everyone should read, it was horrifying and fascinating. Lisa felt just like reading a horror story now; she needed strong stuff to take her mind off her own troubles. But she was disappointed as soon as she'd opened the book. To begin with, she saw from a glance at the introduction that this wasn't a made-up story, it was the diary of a real life girl. Which meant that it was going to be dead boring. She read the first page and saw at once that it was just the stupid, day-to-day sort of stuff about a silly little girl's birthday presents that she might have expected. She put it back on the shelf.

Laurent and Pierre and Alice came back late in the afternoon, pleased with themselves. Pierre and Alice had been accepted at the French school, the Lycée, and were to start at once. They'd had lunch in a French restaurant and gone to a French film. They told Fanny about it over the evening meal, all talking at once and very fast. Lisa didn't understand a word, until Laurent said, 'Speak in English, if you please.'

Pierre scowled. Alice protested rapidly, in French, so that

[41]

Lisa had no idea what she was saying. Laurent repeated, 'In English. It is not polite to talk in a language which not everyone understands.'

This time Pierre did not look at Lisa, but she knew what he was thinking. Only the French knew what manners should be. She was angry again. She didn't listen to the descriptions of the school or the film.

Term started. The new school was both worse and better than Lisa had feared. It was difficult to find her way around the huge new building. More than once she got lost and was in trouble for being late for a lesson. She had to get used to new teachers as well as new class mates. But she was finding life easier, now that she and Pierre and Alice were out for the whole of every weekday. At the weekends, Fanny had planned expeditions for them all together, but they were not a success, and before long she gave up the attempt. It was disappointing. She had hoped that after the first shock, Lisa would find that having a brother and sister made up for whatever she had lost in being an only child. But the autumn glowed and faded, and still Lisa had that buttoned-up look that showed her displeasure, and Pierre and Alice were behaving as if they were visitors in the house, elaborately polite and, with Fanny, uncommunicative.

'Do they talk to you?' Fanny asked Laurent one evening when they were alone.

'Sometimes. Alice talks more than Pierre. He has always been a silent one.'

'I worry about them. I'd so hoped they'd settle down here with us and feel as if it was really their home.'

'Give them time. They have been in the country for a few months only. Remember how different everything is for them. New people, new city, new school, new family. You must not expect them to behave as if they had lived here for ever.'

'Are they homesick? Do they tell you?'

'They have not said so.' But Laurent remembered that

Alice, the day before, had said, 'When I'm grown up I shall go back to France and live there always.' He said, 'Of course they miss some things they were used to. In Paris.'

'Their mother?' Fanny asked.

'Probably. Though she never saw much of them. She had her work, you see, even when they were babies. There was always a *bonne* – a nurse, or a governess to take care of them.'

'They ought to see her sometimes, though. They mustn't grow up not knowing at all what she's like. They should go to Paris to visit her sometimes.'

'It will be difficult to arrange,' Laurent said.

'She must want to see them occasionally! Even if she doesn't want them living with her, surely she doesn't mean to give them up for good?'

'Perhaps you should meet Marie-Louise,' was Laurent's next remark.

'You mean I don't know what she's like?'

'You don't have an idea. She is very . . . grown-up.'

'Aren't I grown-up?'

'In some ways. But Marie-Louise is all grown-up. She hasn't anything childish about her. She has forgotten what it is like to be a child, so children annoy her. She would like them to behave like adults all the time. She can't wait for Pierre and Alice to grow up.'

'That's horrible! Poor kids!' Fanny said.

'Not so poor now they have you.'

'But I'm not any good for them. I can't get near them. It's as if there was a glass wall between us. I don't feel I know what they're really like, or what they want, what they're feeling, or anything.'

'It will get better, I promise you.'

'And Lisa doesn't help. She's still behaving as if they were visitors whom she doesn't much like.'

'They have not had another fight?'

'No. But they're not friendly. It's a sort of cold war.'

'Well! A cold war is better than a hot one,' Laurent said.

But the next day, the cold war ended and the hot war began.

9

The first skirmishes were, unusually, between Laurent and Fanny.

Breakfast was just finished. Laurent had gone to work, Alice and Pierre had already left for school and Lisa was putting together her packed lunch. Fanny had cleared the kitchen table and spread out her drawings, when the front door was suddenly opened again and Laurent burst in.

'Sorry to disturb you, *chérie*, but I have found I have no money. Can you lend me ten pounds?' But as he spoke, the wind rushed in through the two open doors and the sheets Fanny was working on swirled off the table like a gigantic paper snowstorm, ending up mostly on the floor.

'Now look what you've done! Why couldn't you shut the door?' Fanny said, enraged.

'I'm sorry. I would help you to sort them, but I have to be in the office in half an hour. May I have the money? Your purse is here?'

'On the dresser. All right, take it. But shut the door first!' Fanny said, as another gust of wind scattered more papers. Laurent turned back to the door, and as he did so, Fanny's purse fell out of his hand, and money as well as paper scattered all over the floor.

Laurent swore. Fanny said, 'Damn you! You did that on purpose! Go on, take the money and get out!' After he'd gone, and she had collected and sorted out the manuscripts and her sketches, she was too angry to work. She made herself coffee, then decided to go out for the day. She would go to the museum and look up the clothes and the furniture of the period she was working on, and give up all pretence that she was calm enough to concentrate on drawing. By the afternoon, she would feel better, and would be able to think about the illustration which had been interrupted earlier.

This was how it happened that when they came back from school, the kitchen was still covered in paper, and Lisa and Pierre and Alice were told to take their tea up to their own rooms. Lisa did some of her homework, got bored and decided that she was going to take time off to read the magazine which her friend Jilly had lent her. Three quarters of an hour later, she came round from a trance of day-dreaming, to realize that it was nearly supper time and she still had at least an hour's work to do.

She heard a car stop outside and looked down. Laurent was home. She heard first the front door and then the door into the kitchen, open and shut. There was a minute or two of quiet talk, then the voices were raised. Laurent and Fanny were shouting at each other. She heard the scrape of a chair, pushed back hastily, then, after another pause, the kitchen door was slammed and footsteps came quickly up the stairs. She heard Fanny go into her bedroom and slam that door too.

'They're quarrelling,' Lisa thought. She realized that she was pleased. If Laurent and Fanny quarrelled badly, would they separate? Would he take his horrible kids away? Of course if that happened, Fanny would be sorry at first, but Lisa would comfort her and soon perhaps she would settle down to the life they'd had before she had met Laurent, and she'd see that it was what they both wanted.

Lisa hoped that it was a really dreadful quarrel. Fanny had a fine temper when she was roused, and if he had one to match, it was quite possible that they wouldn't be able to make it up again. Cheered by this thought, Lisa went back to her homework. She heard her mother go down the stairs and into the kitchen. With any luck supper would be late, and she'd have time to finish her maths before she was called down to eat.

Supper was over an hour late, and it was an uncomfortable meal. Laurent had cooked it, and the food was delicious, but it was clear that the quarrel was still not resolved. Laurent asked Pierre one or two questions, then fell silent. Fanny did not speak at all. The quarrel must have been even worse than Lisa had imagined. Perhaps they had already agreed to part. Lisa noticed that when Fanny left the room at the end of the meal, still without speaking, she took the big portfolio of drawings which was usually kept on a shelf in the kitchen and a pile of papers under her arm. But if she and Laurent separated, surely it wouldn't be Fanny who would move out? Lisa had a moment of panic, foreseeing herself left behind with these hostile foreigners, while her mother fled from an intolerable marriage. Then she remembered that the house belonged to Fanny. When the breakup came, it would be the others who went away.

Laurent told the three children to clear the table and wash up. 'I made the food, now you can work,' he said and left the kitchen. Pierre started washing the dishes and Lisa, not wanting to share anything with Alice, and encouraged by the thought that neither she nor Pierre might be around for much longer, went to stand by the sink, ready to dry. She looked at Pierre sideways and thought that he was quite good looking, and surprised herself by wondering if, when he'd gone, she would miss him. If he hadn't almost always behaved as if she wasn't there, she might have been able to put up with him. She might even have liked him. Now that he would soon be leaving, she felt almost friendly towards him.

He washed industriously and she dried. Plates, mugs, knives, forks, spoons. Lisa said, 'You're a very fast washer up.'

'Please?' he said.

'I said, you wash up very fast.'

'I am too fast? You cannot dry up so fast?'

'It isn't "dry up", it's just "dry". "Dry up" means something different.'

'What does it mean?'

'To stop. Stop speaking.'

'So if I say to you, "Now dry up", it means you should not speak?'

'That's right.'

'I shall remember,' Pierre said.

'It's not a very polite way of telling someone to shut up,' Lisa said.

'Then I shall be careful I do not say it to you.'

She didn't want him to not be polite to her, but at the same time she wished he wasn't so careful. She said, 'I'll never have to say it to you. You don't talk to me.'

'Do you wish that I should?'

'I don't like it when you pretend I'm not there.'

'When do I do this?'

'When I'm in the same room and you behave as if I wasn't.'

He took the last plate out of the soapy water and rinsed it before he answered that. Then he said, 'Your mother and my father, they were pretending this tonight.'

Lisa didn't know what to say to this. She was surprised when he said next, 'There has been a quarrel, don't you think?'

Lisa played stupid. 'Who's had a quarrel?'

'Laurent and Fanny. They are angry just now.'

He seemed to be taking it very lightly, as if arguments between married couples happened every day. She said, 'My Mum's furious. She may have decided she can't go on like this.'

'She will not continue to be furious? My father will not be angry for long either.'

'I didn't mean that. I mean she may decide the marriage isn't any good.'

Pierre laughed. 'She will not say that for a little quarrel.

[48]

People who are married quarrel all the time. No, not all the time, but often. How could they be together without quarrels?'

'People in England don't.'

'Perhaps they quarrel where you don't hear them. How do you know if your mother quarrelled with your father? You don't remember.'

'Did Laurent and your mother quarrel?' She wouldn't have been surprised if he had refused to answer, but he said, easily, 'I am sure when they first were married. But not before they had the divorce. Then, if they were together, they did not speak. It was . . . disagreeable.'

Alice interrupted in quick French sentences which Lisa couldn't understand. Pierre answered, also in French. Lisa said impatiently, 'What's the matter?'

'She does not like that I tell you about our mother.'

'You haven't told me anything,' Lisa said. To Alice, she said, 'I don't want to know about your mother.' She would have liked to add, 'I know she doesn't want you living with her, that's all.' But something stopped her saying it. However much you disliked some people, there were still one or two things you didn't say to them. Things that were so hurtful that it would be like plunging in a dagger.

It was curious, that because she knew how much she could hurt Pierre and Alice and because she hadn't done it, she felt friendlier towards them than she had before. Friendlier, perhaps, to Pierre, and even towards Alice she felt slightly less hostile. When they had finished clearing the kitchen, Lisa would have liked either of the other two – but preferably Pierre – to suggest that they should do something together. They could have wanted to watch a programme on television or to play a game. But Pierre left the room with Alice, without saying more than 'Good night' in his usual neutral tone. So he didn't really want to be friendly. Lisa almost wished she had used the dagger after all.

*

She was anxious about her mother's intentions for the rest of the evening. She even wondered if she could have left the house already. Before going to bed, she tapped on her mother's door and, when there was no answer, looked in. Fanny was lying on her bed, but not asleep. She turned her head as Lisa came into the room, and said, 'Go to bed, love. It's late.'

'I just wanted to say good night.'

'Good night. Sleep well.'

So she was not going to tell Lisa about her plans for the future. But at least she was still there.

Breakfast the next morning was, as usual for the children, a hurried meal. Today Lisa wasn't quite certain that she did want Laurent to leave. It wasn't Laurent whom she objected to; if only Fanny could tell him, 'Laurent, I'm afraid I can't have Pierre and Alice here any longer. They upset Lisa and they don't fit in. They will have to go back to their mother, whether she likes it or not.' After all, children ought to be with their mother, and she ought to want to have them. By the end of the school day, Lisa had arranged everything satisfactorily in her mind, and was ready to be given the good news.

Her first surprise when she reached home ten yards ahead of Alice and Pierre, was to find the kitchen empty. No Fanny, surrounded by papers, saying distractedly, 'Get your own teas, kids, and don't talk.' But before she had had time to panic that this time Fanny had really left, she heard herself called. 'Lisa! Come up to my room, will you? I want to talk to you.'

This was it. She was to be told of the new arrangements.

'Shut the door. I'll talk to the others later. But as you're the person most concerned, I wanted to tell you first.' That was just the opening she might have expected. Her mother was standing by the window that overlooked the garden, and Lisa could tell by her voice and by her restlessness, that she was anxious.

'Lisa, I know you're not going to like this, and I'm sorry. It isn't how I'd meant things to be.'

Fanny hesitated. Lisa said, 'Never mind, Mum. I'm sure it'll be all right.' She meant to be comforting, and she was surprised when her mother said sharply, 'You don't know what I'm going to say!'

'Go on, then.'

'I've decided . . . This arrangement isn't any good. I can't go on working in the kitchen. I must have somewhere of my own.'

'You're going away? You mean, you're leaving?'

'Of course I'm not. It's just that I need more room. Somewhere where I can leave my work spread out if I need to.'

'Can't you get a studio somewhere?'

'It'd cost more than I could earn. I've decided, I've got to go back to the room that used to be my workroom.'

'Where Alice is? Is she going, then?' Getting rid of one of the intruders wasn't as good as their both leaving, but it was still good news.

'Of course she's not going. Don't be stupid, Lisa. You and she will have to share.'

Lisa couldn't believe that she'd heard aright. Her mother could not possibly mean what she'd said.

'I won't! I won't have that horrible little . . . rat . . . in with me! It's my room! It's always been mine!'

'I'm sorry. I knew you wouldn't like it . . .'

'I hate it! I won't have her in my room. I'd rather die than have her there!'

'Lisa, be sensible. There isn't anywhere else she can sleep, and your room's quite large enough for two.'

'Why can't she share with Pierre?'

'Because he's a boy and she's a girl. They're too old to be sharing a room.'

'She could sleep in the kitchen. Or the living room.' But she knew that this wasn't a serious possibility.

'Don't be stupid! I really am sorry, love. If there was any other way of managing it, I wouldn't ask you to share with Alice . . .'

'You're not asking! You haven't given me a choice!'

'No. There isn't any choice. I'm afraid that's how it's got to be,' Fanny said.

'Why can't you go on working in the kitchen? You said you thought it would be all right.'

'I can't because it isn't all right. Having to clear the table for meals all the time is absolutely impossible. I must have somewhere where I can leave my drawings spread out, so that I know exactly where I am. I'm wasting hours, this way, and I can't afford to. I'm badly late with this last commission now, and if this goes on, no one will want to give me any work.'

'You don't have to work, do you? Can't Laurent give you more money?'

'No, he can't. I need to work just as much as I ever did.'

'Why can't Alice go back to her real mother? We don't want her here.'

'You know why. I've explained about Alice's mother. And anyway, Laurent wants to have his children with him, just as I want to have you.'

'If you really wanted to have me, you wouldn't do this. You knew I'd hate it. I don't want to share with anyone, and I don't want stinking Alice in the house, even.'

'I've said I'm sorry. I know it's hard on you.'

'I won't have her! I won't!'

Fanny and Lisa stared at each other. There was a moment's silence, then Fanny said, 'I thought we could put her bed over against the left-hand wall and I'll try to rig up a curtain between you so that it'll seem more like having a room to yourself.'

'I'll be able to hear everything she does,' Lisa said, though what she really meant was that Alice would be able to hear everything she herself did.

[52]

'I don't suppose Alice will be any better pleased than you are,' Fanny said.

'I don't care whether she is or not.'

'You might think that it's going to be worse for her, being put in with someone who doesn't really like her, and in a strange place.'

'She's lucky to be here,' Lisa said.

'Well? Haven't you been lucky, never having to share anything with anyone before? I know this arrangement is hard on you, and I'll try to think of some way round it, but for the moment you've just got to put up with it.'

'When . . .?'

'I'm going to ask Alice to move her things out of the little room tomorrow. By then I hope I'll have organized the curtain.'

'You haven't told her yet?' Lisa asked.

'No. I've told you first. I just hope she won't make as much fuss about it as you,' Fanny said, then wished she hadn't. She wasn't surprised that Lisa banged out of the room, slamming the door behind her.

10

When Lisa came back from school the next afternoon, and went into her room, she saw that the move had already been made. A thick dark green curtain cut off the left-hand side of the room, and the wardrobe had been moved so that it was now at the end of her bed. The desk at which she did her homework was no longer between the two windows, but was next to the bed head. She looked behind the curtain and saw Alice's bed and the painted chest of drawers which had been in her mother's workroom. There were new hooks on the wall, and Alice's dresses were hanging there. Lisa stood for a minute, hating the whole scene.

She heard Alice's steps on the stairs and went back to her own half room. When Alice came in at the door, she said, 'You'll have to come in through my part of the room, but you're never to stop here.'

'*Je ne le veux pas*,' Alice said.

'And I'm not talking to you? Understand? Comprenez?'

'*Je comprends. Moi aussi, je ne veux pas parler. Ni moi non plus.*'

'Don't understand,' Lisa said, deliberately stupid.

'*Ça ne me fait rien.*' Alice said, and disappeared behind the curtain.

'I'm going to behave exactly as if she wasn't there,' Lisa thought. But this was more difficult than she'd expected. She found that she was yawning more loudly, scraping back her chair on the floor more aggressively, turning up her radio, the accompaniment to which she always did her homework, louder than she would have if there'd been no one else in the room. It was impossible to concentrate. And it was infuriating that Alice was being so quiet. When Lisa turned off the radio and listened, she could hear nothing. Alice seemed not even to be breathing. Lisa wanted to look, to see what she was doing there so noiselessly, but it was below her dignity to be curious. She couldn't concentrate. She knew that she was working badly, and that was another black mark against Alice. When she was in bed that night, she hoped she'd be kept awake by Alice's snoring, which would have been reason enough for a legitimate complaint, but the darkness was not disturbed by any sound from the other side of the curtain.

The half term week approached, and at breakfast one Saturday, Laurent asked what the family wanted to do.

'I could take an extra day or two off and we could go to Paris for the weekend. Would you like that?' He was speaking to Fanny and Lisa as well as his own children.

'It'd be wonderful! But the expense!' Fanny said, at the same moment as Alice was exclaiming, '*Merveilleux! Fantastique!*' and Pierre, more soberly, asked, 'Where should we be lodging?'

'Jean-Paul's flat is empty just now. We could all sleep there. We would go by train and across the Channel by boat. It would not cost very much,' Laurent said.

'Perfect! I've always wanted to take Lisa to Paris. Don't you think it'd be fun, love?' Fanny asked Lisa.

Go to Paris with the others? Go to a city that Pierre and Alice knew already and she didn't know at all? A country where they'd be able to jabber away to everyone they met, and she wouldn't be able to say a word? Lisa said, 'No thanks, I don't want to go,' and was spitefully pleased to see her mother's face fall. She saw too, that Pierre and Alice looked at each other in congratulation, and perversely she was tempted to disappoint them by changing her decision.

'Lisa! You'd enjoy it! Remember how we used to plan running off there by ourselves without telling anyone? This would be even better, because we'll have Laurent to take us around.'

How could her mother be so stupid? Lisa wondered. How was it that she couldn't see that exploring Paris, just the two of them together, would have been quite different from trailing about with Laurent and Pierre and horrible Alice, all probably showing off how well they knew the city. She said, 'You can all go without me. I'd rather stay here.'

'You can't stay here alone,' Fanny said.

'Mum! I'm nearly twelve! I'm quite old enough.'

'No. You'll come with us. And I don't want any argument.'

Lisa waited until the meal was over. Then she caught her mother alone and said, 'I really don't want to go to Paris, Mum. Can't I go and stay with Grandma and Grandpa? I'm sure they'd have me.'

'I expect they would. But I wanted us all to do something together,' Fanny said.

'It'd save money if you didn't have to take me too.'

'I'd rather spend the extra and have you with us.'

'But if I really don't want to?'

'Lisa, love, it would be an adventure. You've never been to a big capital city abroad. There are lots of lovely things to see, and the food is wonderful.'

'I'd rather have Grandma's food. Anyway, I want to see them again.'

'Very well. If you're quite sure. But Lisa, if they say yes, then that's it. You can't change your mind afterwards and decide you'd rather come with us.'

'I shan't change my mind. I know I don't want to go to Paris.'

It was a wonderful relief at first to be in Grandpa's and Grandma's quiet house. It was wonderful to have a room to herself, and to be the only child around, having her preferences in food consulted, and being as nearly spoiled as was possible with someone like her grandma. It was peaceful here, with no rivals. Lisa wished she could stay for ever.

The place reminded her of something she'd almost forgotten. When she was alone with her grandmother after supper on Monday evening, she asked, 'If it was too dangerous for Grandpa to go back to Vienna that time when he was staying here, why didn't his mother and father and his sister come and stay in England too?'

'I don't think they had any idea of what was going to happen in their country.'

'Did Grandpa know?'

'He didn't know for certain. Someone did warn him, but it didn't seem like sense at the time.'

'Why didn't whoever it was warn the others too? Or Grandpa could have told them.'

'I don't think it would have made any difference. People often don't believe what they don't want to. Lisa, if you've finished drying the silver, will you please put it away in the cutlery drawer? You know how it fits in, don't you?'

Lisa did. While she slotted spoons into spoons and forks into forks, still thinking about the family which had been left behind in Vienna, she began asking, 'Did you ever see Grandpa's . . .' when her grandmother interrupted her.

'You know you told me what Pierre said about mirrors? When you wrote to me after you'd been staying here?'

'You mean about them being doors?' She was uncomfortable.

'I've remembered where he got it from. It was *Orphée*.'

'What's *Orphée*?'

'It was a very good French film about Orpheus, the musician, the poet, in the Greek myth. One of the characters in the film says that mirrors are doors. You actually see Death coming through a mirror.'

She didn't really want to hear, but she found herself asking, 'Why?'

'Because the story about Orpheus is that his wife dies and he goes down into the underworld to find her and to bring her back. In this film, he goes through the mirror too.'

'He couldn't. Could he? Not really.'

'I suppose it's trick photography. It's very well done. If the film comes round some time, I'll try to take you to see it.'

'Does he bring her back?'

'I suppose so. The story in the film isn't exactly like the Greek story.'

'Why does Death come through the mirror?'

'You'll understand when you see the film. What were you going to ask me just now?'

'I don't know. What did I say?'

'You started asking me if I'd ever seen something.'

Now she remembered. 'Did you ever see Grandpa's sister? The one who died.'

'Of course I did. When the family was living in London we all played together in the Square garden.'

'Did you like her?'

'Yes. We were very good friends.'

'Was she like Grandpa?'

'Not at all like him in character. She had a temper. She used to fly out at you if she didn't like what you were doing or something you said. But she was very affectionate, too. I remember . . .'

'What?' Lisa asked.

'I remember how surprised I was when I first got to know her. She wasn't like the English children I'd known. She'd rush up and kiss me when we met and I wasn't used to that. I've got some old photographs somewhere. I'm pretty sure there'll be one of Elsbet. I'll show you when we've finished clearing up,' her grandmother was saying.

The old photographs were black and white and small and faded. And all the people in them were unrecognizable.

'Why did they wear such ugly things?' Lisa asked.

'That was what everyone wore then. Look, that's Grandpa and that's me,' her grandmother said, pointing to the figures of a small boy in unfamiliar knicker-bockers and a smaller girl with a plait of hair over each shoulder. They were standing in a garden. Lisa could see bushes and trees in the background.

'How old were you then?' she asked.

'John must have been nine or ten, and I was about six.'

'You're wearing a dress! Didn't you ever wear jeans?'

'Girls didn't in those days. It was skirts all the time. Except sometimes when we were by the sea. I think there's a photo, somewhere here of me in Cornwall, wearing a pair of Tom's old shorts.'

She hunted among the pile of snapshots. Lisa picked up one or two, trying to guess which of her grown-up relatives this fat baby or that sulky looking teenager might have been. Among the small, curling oblongs were several much larger ones, mounted on stiff board by a professional hand. Lisa turned one over and saw the head and shoulders of a serious young woman with a great deal of hair and an old-fashioned dress. Grandpa's mother, she guessed. She picked up another. A cold finger touched her spine.

'Grandma! Who's this?'

'That? Oh, that's Elsbet. Grandpa's little sister.'

Lisa was looking at the picture of a girl of seven or eight, dressed in what was obviously her best velvet dress, facing the camera. Her mouth was set in a straight line, as if she had been determined not to smile when the photographer told her to.

'Lisa? What's the matter?'

Lisa managed to say, 'Nothing.'

'I expect I've got some more of her among all these others. That one's too stiff. She didn't really look as serious as that most of the time.'

Lisa's grandmother sorted the snapshots. Lisa was grateful that she wasn't looking at her. At intervals she said, 'Here's another of John. Here's one of my mother, it's terrible, she always came out badly. This is the house we lived in. That's me going to a fancy dress party ... Lisa, there is something wrong! What is it? Don't you feel well?'

It was a relief to say that she didn't. Lisa allowed herself to be put to bed. The thermometer under her tongue meant that she did not need to talk. She couldn't wait to be left alone in the dark room, hugging the unnecessary but comforting hot water bottle. But she knew she wouldn't be able to go to sleep for hours. She had to try to work out how it was that now she herself had seen a ghost.

11

The little girl she had seen in that photograph was the child she had seen in the double mirror image. She had seen Elsbet alive. But Elsbet had died years ago. If she'd been alive now, she'd have been nearly as old as Grandpa. Lisa had seen her ghost.

She had been lighthearted when she'd been trying to find out about the ghost her grandparents might or might not have seen. Now she felt different. She was frightened. How could she have seen someone who had been alive before the World War, more than sixty years ago? And how could she have believed that that person had seen her, had spoken to her? It didn't make sense. Lisa wondered if perhaps she was going mad.

She fell asleep eventually long after she had heard the twelve strokes of midnight from the clock in the hall downstairs. When she came down late to breakfast the next morning, her grandmother exclaimed at her appearance.

'Are you sure you're fit to be up, Lisa? You don't look well.'

'I'm all right,' Lisa said.

'Tea? Or would you prefer coffee this morning? I'm just going to have my mid-morning cup, so it would be no trouble to make another.'

Lisa chose tea. Hot, strong, sweet tea was what she needed. She had to find a way of asking the questions she wanted answered, without alarming Grandma, and without giving away her own fears.

'Grandma, when you saw the ghost boy . . .'

'I told you, I don't believe he was really a ghost.'

'Grandpa thinks he was.'

Lisa's grandmother did not answer this. 'Have some toast, Lisa. I'll make you some fresh.'

'I'm not hungry.'

'I don't believe you are quite well. Let me feel your forehead.' But the forehead proved to be reassuringly cool, and Lisa went on with her questions.

'Why did Grandpa's sister stay in Austria if it wasn't safe there? She did stay, didn't she?'

'It's difficult for us to understand, now that we know what happened afterwards. I don't think John's family thought of there being actual danger for themselves. And Elsbet was quite young. She was only eight or nine when the war started. I daresay her parents thought she was too young to send away by herself.'

'But they could all have gone somewhere safe.'

'It isn't that easy to pack up and leave everything you've known and to go to live in a strange land, with no money and no job and probably nowhere to live.'

'I thought they had plenty of money.'

'After Hitler had taken over, people who wanted to leave Austria weren't allowed to take more than a few pounds with them. Nothing like enough to live on here.'

'Who paid for Grandpa, then?'

'I think it was the family he stayed with. The Jessels. You've met Marietta. She was the younger sister of Nicky, Grandpa's schoolfriend. She came here once when you were staying with us, with her two little girls. Don't you remember? Stella and Kitty. A bit younger than you. Here's your tea.'

Lisa said 'Thanks' and was grateful for the chance to think up her next question, while she sipped the tea. It did make her feel better.

'Have you ever known anyone who's gone mad?' she asked next.

'Lisa, can't you think about something more agreeable? First it's ghosts and now it's madness. No, I haven't, I'm glad to say.'

'Can you go mad suddenly? After you've been quite all right to begin with?'

'What's all this about, Lisa? Do you know someone you think is going mad?'

It was an easy way out. 'There's a girl at school I'm not sure about. She says funny things.'

'What sort of funny? I suppose you mean funny peculiar, not funny ha ha.'

'She said she'd seen someone who wasn't really there.'

'What do you mean, wasn't really there?'

'If she looked one way, she could see her, but if she looked the other way, she couldn't. And then she discovered that it was a real person who'd been dead a long time.'

'So that's why you've been talking about ghosts! I don't think you realize the sort of tricks some people's imaginations play on them.'

'She didn't make it up,' Lisa said.

'I don't expect she meant to. But plenty of people can persuade themselves they've seen something mysterious without using their common sense. If you're really worried about your friend at school you should talk to one of the teachers. Does she behave in an odd way apart from seeing things that aren't there?'

Lisa said, 'No, she's all right except for that,' and hoped that this was true. She didn't think she was behaving strangely. But she certainly felt strange. She had seen Elsbet's ghost and a room she'd never been in. She was frightened. She had almost made up her mind never to look in a mirror again.

12

When she was back in London, the problems of sharing a room with Alice became too important for Lisa to think about anything else. For the time being, she almost forgot that she might have seen a ghost. She was dealing now with a very much alive girl.

It was infuriating that Alice did almost nothing that Lisa could complain about. She kept to her side of the dividing curtain except when she had to come past it in order to reach the door. She did not disturb Lisa in the night. She never complained of Lisa's bedside light however late Lisa kept it on. She moved quietly. What Lisa couldn't bear was that she was always there. Her quietness was like a threat, as if she'd been saying, 'I'm here, listening. You won't hear me, but I can hear you. I shall know everything you do. You're never going to be alone again.'

Lisa went into attack. She turned up the volume of music on her radio so that she herself could hardly bear it.

'Please not so loud. It disturbs my working,' Alice said from the other side of the curtain.

'You ought to learn to work against a noise. You can't always be in a place where it's absolutely quiet,' Lisa said.

'Could you please listen with those things for the ears? Then I would not hear so well.'

'Earphones, they're called. No, I can't, they're broken.'

'Then please make it . . . feebler . . . so I don't hear it.'

'Feeble's what you are,' Lisa said, and turned the sound down as little as she could. The next day, Pierre said to her, 'Why do you have music when you are working?'

'It helps me to concentrate.'

'Anyone would find it impossible to work with that noise in the same room.'

'Then they shouldn't stay in the room,' Lisa said.

That evening, the silence in her bedroom seemed more marked than ever. She worked for a time, stopping sometimes to listen for the creak of Alice's chair or the scratching of her pen. But there was nothing. At last she looked behind the curtain. Alice was not there. When they were called down to supper, Lisa saw Alice come out of Pierre's room, carrying books and paper. So she'd been doing her homework with him. It might have been a triumph, but Lisa did not feel triumphant.

She knew she was being disagreeable. To everyone, not just to Alice and Pierre. She knew, too, that her mother was deliberately not asking her what was wrong. Fanny knew. Lisa did once say, 'Couldn't Alice sleep in the workroom after you've finished there?' and Fanny had said, 'No, she can't. I'm often working there till after ten at night. You've got to put up with sharing. Most people of your age do.'

'That's with real sisters. Alice isn't my sister!'

'If you were at boarding school, you'd be sharing with complete strangers,' Fanny said.

'But it wouldn't ever have been my room that I'm used to being alone in.'

'I know it's hard, and I've said I'm sorry. Alice doesn't disturb you, does she? She's not a noisy child.'

'It's just her being there that I don't like.'

'I'm afraid you've got to get used to it. If we ever have enough money to build a studio at the end of the garden . . .'

'Will you ever?'

'I'm afraid it's a long way off,' Fanny said.

It was the second half of the autumn term. Christmas was approaching. Though she wouldn't have admitted it, Lisa was getting used to sharing her room. In fact, the sharing was only at night; during the day Alice was practically never there. Lisa found that she could entertain her friends in her own room without fear that Alice was the other side of the curtain, listening to everything they said. Alice spent almost all her waking hours at home in Pierre's room or the kitchen. She became, as far as Lisa was concerned, very nearly invisible. But this convenient behaviour, Lisa knew, was not the result of friendliness or wanting to please her. Alice was her enemy. Lisa wouldn't have wished it otherwise. If Alice hated her, that made it all right for her to hate Alice.

'What are we going to do for Christmas?' she asked her mother on a cold dark evening at the end of November.

'Grandma and Grandpa would like us all to go there for the weekend.'

'Who's all?' she asked, suspicious.

'All of us. You and me and Laurent and Alice and Pierre.'

'There wouldn't be room,' Lisa said at once.

'Grandma thinks she could squash us all in. Alice and you in the spare room over the kitchen, and Pierre would have to sleep in the living room on the sofa bed.'

'If he can do that in Grandma's house, why can't he sleep in the living room here?'

'He can there because it'll only be for two or three nights and it won't matter how late he goes to bed because he hasn't got to get to school in the morning.'

'Can't it be me that sleeps in the living room?'

'No, it can't. Lisa, I wish you'd stop making difficulties about everything. Wouldn't it be fun to spend Christmas in the country with Grandma and Grandpa? You've always loved it before.'

'That was when it was just you and me.'

'You mean you'd rather stay here, in London?'

'Would it be with them here too?'

'Of course it would. I want them to be with us for their first Christmas since their family split up. It's going to be difficult for them.'

'It's difficult for me!' Lisa said.

Fanny began, 'Don't be so . . .' then broke off and said, more gently, 'I know it is. But I think it would be easier for everyone if we were in a different place. And having Grandma and Grandpa around will help. Try not to make up your mind that you're not going to enjoy it. Sometimes being part of a big family can be wonderful.'

It won't be for me, Lisa thought, and told herself how much she didn't want to share Grandma and Grandpa with Alice and Pierre. Grandpa would be able to talk French to them. He and Grandma might like them better than Lisa. No. Not Grandma. She would certainly take Lisa's side, but Grandpa might well tell Lisa that she was behaving badly, or say that she was being stupid about them, which was, for Grandpa, a worse accusation.

Thinking about her grandparents reminded Lisa of what she hadn't forgotten, but hadn't wanted to think about. Ghosts.

It was the end of a December afternoon, dark and cold. Lisa went into her mother's bedroom and sat down in front of the dressing table. She examined the reflection it gave her back; her own head and shoulders against the background of the shaded room. Outside the window the branches of the trees were black against the rapidly darkening sky. She picked up the hand mirror. When she looked into it, it too reflected back her own face. She thought, I've been frightened of nothing, it's just an ordinary mirror. To prove it, she made herself turn her back on the large mirror and hold up the smaller glass so that she could see the double reflection.

She saw dark hair. The back of her own head. Now if she turned half sideways, she would see her unfamiliar profile. But before she could do this, the head in the mirror had moved and she was looking at a face which was not her own. Now she recognized the small girl she had seen before with the kitten, and around her was the same room with the

[67]

dark furniture and the shelf of silver-framed photographs and the table with its embroidered runner. But today the flowers in the vase at its centre were not pale but dark. Dark crimson.

She wanted to step away. She wanted to have nothing to do with this reflected room, this double image ghost. But she was curious as well as frightened. She knew now how to enter that other life. She stepped backwards, turned and found herself standing face to face with the child who was Elsbet.

'You were here before,' Elsbet said.

'You pulled me. Through the mirror,' Lisa said.

'That mirror? Then it is true what Hans says.'

'Who's Hans?'

'My brother is Hans. He says that only ghosts can pass through mirrors. So you are a ghost.'

'No, I'm not! I'm alive. You're the ghost, because you're dead.'

'You are *dumm* . . . stupid. I am living here in our apartment. Of course I am not dead.'

'Where are we? I mean, where is this apartment?' Lisa asked. But she did not understand Elsbet's answer.

'I thought you lived in London,' Lisa said.

'We were living in London till last year. Now we are back in . . .' It sounded like 'Veen'.

'Where's Veen?'

'*Wien*. You would say Vienna. Here, where we are now.'

'Is your brother here too?'

'Hans?'

'Not Hans. John, he's called.'

'They are the same. Hans is the short name for Johann. Hans is here.'

'He ought to go back to London. He oughtn't to stay here. There's going to be a war.'

'You can't know this. There won't be any war.'

'Yes, there will be. I know.'

[68]

'You are only a stupid boy that tells lies.'

'I'm not a boy and I'm not telling lies. I know about it because I don't belong here, in this time. I'm really alive in the future. So I know about the war that's going to happen to you. It's sort of history to me.' It was a muddled explanation and she was not surprised that Elsbet didn't understand it.

'This is a nonsense. You are telling this to frighten me.'

'No, it's true. You've got to believe me . . .'

'Why should I believe you when you say what I know is not true?'

Lisa lost what remained of her temper. 'You silly little girl, why don't you listen? I do know what's going to happen to you, because I'm alive years later than you. There's going to be a war and you're going to get killed. If you had any sense, you'd try to escape, but if you don't listen to me, you won't be able to.'

Several things seemed to happen at once. Elsbet threw herself against the door of the room and began to call out. *'Mutti! Mutti! Komm schnell, hier ist ein verrückter Knabe!'* At the same moment another door opened and Fanny was saying, 'What in the world . . .? I've been looking all over for you.' Lisa found herself stepping forwards out of – what? – and saying, 'I just wanted to look in your long mirror.'

'I don't know how you think you can see anything without any light! I wanted to tell you that Laurent's going to take us all out for a grand meal in a restaurant this evening. He's got the commission he wanted and we're going to celebrate.'

Lisa put the hand mirror down on the dressing table. She looked into the big mirror and saw only her mother and herself, real, ordinary and safe. She was utterly confused.

13

The days just before Christmas passed in the usual turmoil. Lisa was grateful that there was so little time to think.

'Have you got a headache?' her mother asked her.

'No. Why?'

'You don't look quite right. And you're not eating properly.'

'I'm all right, Mum. Really.'

'Are you getting on better with Alice now? I noticed you've been doing things with her and Pierre more lately.'

'Not really. I mean, I still don't like her.'

'You would tell me if there was anything wrong, wouldn't you?' Fanny said.

Lisa said, 'Yes.' But she wasn't going to speak to anyone about what she thought she'd seen in the two mirrors. If it hadn't been a dream, and she was sure it hadn't, then she was having what were called hallucinations. Perhaps it would never happen again, and if she didn't tell anyone about it, she would never be suspected of being anything but in her right mind.

There was plenty to think about. She had to decide what Christmas presents she should give Alice and Pierre. She would have to find something for them, however much she didn't want to. Finally, she chose books for them. *Black Beauty* for Alice, which was insulting because it was too young for her and would probably bore her; French children didn't want to read about horses, though they might eat them. For Pierre, she bought a science fiction story which she wouldn't have read herself, but which he might even enjoy. She wasn't going to take the trouble to consult his tastes but this choice seemed safe, neither insultingly young nor flatteringly adult.

On Christmas Day, Lisa handed her presents to Pierre and Alice, and was thanked with no more enthusiasm than they deserved. She was curious as to what they would give her. Alice's present to her was a book; in French, of course. The title meant nothing to her, it was probably something she wouldn't want to read even in English. Pierre's present was so small and beautifully wrapped that for a moment Lisa wondered if he was heaping coals of fire on her by giving her a pair of earrings or a brooch. But it turned out to be ear plugs. 'So that you will not hear noises that keep you awake,' Pierre explained.

'You seem to be getting on quite well with your new brother and sister,' Grandpa said to Lisa, when Christmas and Boxing Day were over and life was nearly ordinary again.

'We get on all right,' Lisa said.

'Yesterday, when we were all playing that game . . . What is its stupid name? . . . I thought you were all quite friendly.'

Lisa said, 'Mm.' She wasn't going to admit to being friendly with Pierre and Alice. But when she was alone with Grandma a day later, she came much nearer to saying what she felt.

'They're very well-behaved children, here, at any rate. Are they like this when you're at home?' Grandma asked.

'They always behave all right when we're with other people,' Lisa said.

'Not with you? Are they still insisting on talking French to you?'

'Not so much.' Lisa did not want to say that when they were alone they did not talk at all.

'So things are a bit better?'

'Not really. Mum's moved Alice into my room and I hate it. I hate having to share.'

[71]

'I'm sorry! There's no other way I could fit you all in here,' her grandmother said.

'I didn't mean here.' But she did. 'I meant at home. It's always been my room, ever since I was born, and now I've got Alice taking up half of it.'

'Is she unpleasant to you there? Noisy? Is that why Pierre gave you those ear plugs?'

'She isn't exactly noisy, it's just that I know she's there all the time, and I like being alone.'

'Being alone is a luxury not many people can enjoy,' Lisa's grandmother said.

'Some people don't like it.'

'Well, I'm sorry you feel like that, but obviously you'll have to put up with it for the present.' Lisa wriggled. She had expected more sympathy than this.

'Are you quite all right again now, Lisa? Fanny said you hadn't been very well just before you came away.'

'I'm fine.' But this reminded her of what she'd almost been able to forget. She decided to ask again, 'What really happened in the war, Grandma?'

'What do you mean, what really happened?'

'What happened to Grandpa's mother and father?'

'I have told you. They died. A long time ago.'

'Was it in that war?'

'Yes.'

'Was it a bomb that our side dropped on their house?'

'Why don't you ask Fanny to tell you what happened? And don't ask Grandpa.'

There was no opportunity in this crowded house to speak to her mother alone. Lisa did her best to forget the whole uncomfortable subject. This wasn't difficult because, except at night, there was seldom time to think. Grandma had established a rota by which everyone helped in the house, and all the tasks were shared, so that there was always someone to talk to as you dusted or peeled potatoes or washed the dishes. When they weren't working, they went on expeditions. They went to a grand house with an enormous garden, which looked thoroughly dead to Lisa, but which Grandpa found fascinating. One day, they drove a long way to a curving shore where the pebbles were like tiny eggs, glistening at the sea's edge as if they were polished. 'The other end of this beach has stones this big,' Grandpa said, his hands far apart to show the size.

'Why? Why are these stones very little here and so large there?' Pierre asked.

'I don't think anyone has explained it exactly. It is the sea that arranges them in this way. They get bigger and bigger, the further east you go. For eighteen miles,' Grandpa said.

'*Fantastique!*' Pierre said.

'I read somewhere that some people believe that if we could look under the sea a little way out, we'd find the pebbles sorted out in the same way but the other way round. The big stones this end and the tiny stones over there by the island.'

'Is it true?' Pierre asked.

'I have no idea. It sounds to me like a story people would like to believe. But one day someone will make an experiment and prove that it is only a story. I shall be sorry. I would rather believe it.'

'But if it isn't true?'

'Don't you sometimes like a mystery?' Grandpa asked. Lisa hadn't been listening with much interest to the conversation, but the word 'mystery' caught her attention. She felt annoyed with both Grandpa and Pierre. Without their knowing it, what they said had forced her mind back to what she didn't want to think about. The room in the mirror, the Elsbet girl, the secret of what had happened to Grandpa's family in the war. Why didn't anyone want to tell her about it? 'No wonder I don't know whether I'm mad or not, everyone's in a plot to keep me from knowing what the truth is,' Lisa thought.

She came back to the present to hear Grandpa say 'What

will you do, Pierre, if you find that all the stones out there under the waves are the same as what we see here? Will you tell me? Or will you let me go on believing in my fairy tale?' Grandpa asked.

'I will tell you, but I will be so . . . gentle . . . that you will not mind.'

'I see. Truth above everything.'

'If you don't know it, then you are making yourself *aveugle*. Blind.'

'You could say I am just enjoying the world of my imagination. After all, I'm not hurting anyone by wondering at the cleverness of the water or the wind, or whatever it is, that arranges the stones in such a . . . such a harmonious way.'

'What about you, Lisa?' her grandmother asked.

'What? I mean, what about me?'

'Do you want to go on believing the story about the stones under the sea? Or are you like Pierre and you want to know what they are really like?'

'I'd want to know what was true,' Lisa said. But she was not thinking about the arrangement of the stones.

'I think it would not be too difficult to discover. If I had a . . .'

'A wet suit,' Laurent said.

'If I had that, I could swim out and look.'

'Not off this beach you couldn't. It's dangerous. No one is allowed to swim here,' Lisa's grandfather said.

'People have been drowned here because they didn't listen to the warnings,' Grandma said.

Warnings. Warning. It was a word Lisa didn't want to think about. Suddenly the wind seemed colder, the shelving shore seemed hostile, the sea, which was grey, ruffled with white, was threatening. She didn't like this conversation. It reminded her of the conversation she had seemed to have had with Elsbet who had died years and years ago. She had tried to warn her of what was going to happen to her, but

[74]

Elsbet hadn't listened. Someone had warned Grandpa and he must have listened or he wouldn't be here now. Who had warned him? Who could have known what was going to happen in that war except someone like Lisa herself, to whom it was history?

She was glad when Grandma said, 'I'm getting cold. Let's go back to the town and find somewhere to have tea. Lisa's shivering.'

She was. But it wasn't only the wind that had chilled her.

14

At the end of the week, they were going back to London. 'Couldn't I stay on a bit with Grandma? School doesn't begin for another week,' Lisa asked her mother.

'No, you can't. Grandma's going to stay with one of her old school friends the day after tomorrow.'

'I could stay with Grandpa, then. I'm sure he'd let me.'

'He might, but I won't. I think he's had enough of the family this last week. He's not used to quite so many people around all the time. He looks tired. And he's paler than usual, not his usual good colour.'

'It'd only be me, and I wouldn't bother him.'

'You wouldn't mean to, but there'd be extra work for him, and I don't want to ask him to do it. I'm sorry, Lisa. But there are lots of things you and the others can do in London. There are always extra shows and exhibitions for children in the Christmas holidays.'

'I don't have to go to things with them. I can go with Jilly.'

'Can't you take them along too? They don't know their way around London as well as you do.'

But when they were at home again, Lisa discovered that there was no question of her doing anything with Pierre and Alice. They disappeared, every morning, directly after breakfast, and did not reappear till late afternoon. She heard Laurent ask them, at supper, what they had done during the day, and heard their descriptions of the places they had visited, the things they had seen. The first time, Laurent said to Lisa, 'Did you go too?' and she had answered, 'No.' She saw her mother look quickly at all three children, but neither she nor Laurent asked any questions. Lisa discovered, to her surprise, that far from enjoying being the only child in the house, she was counting the hours till the evening when the rest of the family would be back. She had never been so horribly bored.

But at least she had Fanny to herself. One day, over their midday meal, she said, 'Mum! I wish you'd tell me why Grandpa won't talk about his family. If there's a secret about what they did, I ought to know.'

'What do you mean, what they did? They didn't do anything they'd have to be secret about.'

'But Grandpa won't talk about them. Grandma doesn't, either.'

Fanny hesitated before she said, 'If you'd been the only person in your family who had escaped being murdered, by an extraordinary piece of luck, wouldn't you feel you didn't want to talk about it?'

'Who was murdered? Grandpa's family?'

'Yes. His mother and his father and his little sister.'

'It wasn't a bomb? I thought perhaps we'd dropped a bomb on their house and that was why Grandpa felt bad about them.'

'It was worse than that. After Hitler had marched into Austria, he did there what he'd been doing in Germany. He got rid of all the people who didn't fit in with his idea of what the German race should be.'

'Got rid of them how?'

'Put them in enormous prisons, called concentration camps, where most of them died.'

'What sort of people?'

'Old people, ill people and gypsies. Anyone who tried to stand up to him. But mostly it was the Jews . . .'

'The Jews? Why? I thought we were Jewish.'

'I am half Jewish, because my father is Jewish. You're a quarter Jewish, because I'm half, and your father wasn't. But you'd have counted as whole Jewish under the Nazis because of having a half Jewish mother.'

'So if we'd lived in Germany, we'd have got killed too?'

'Unless we'd been lucky enough to escape first.'

'Why didn't all the Jews escape before Hitler caught them?'

'Some of them did. But most of them couldn't believe it was going to happen to them. They'd lived in those countries for so long that they thought they really belonged there. Like their friends who weren't Jewish. Sometimes it was those friends who betrayed them.'

Lisa remembered what her grandfather had said. 'Friends can change. You can be frightened of your friends,' he had said.

'Why? What made their friends do that?' she asked.

'Lisa, it's so complicated! John has tried to explain it to me, but I don't know if I really understand. I think sometimes people got frightened for themselves, and they thought they'd be safer if they sided with the Nazi party against the Jews. Because if you were found helping a Jew, hiding him or anything like that, you could get sent to prison too.'

'Ordinary people? Anyone?'

'Anyone. Children. Old people. Babies.'

'Did they have to stay in prison for long?'

'Most of them died there.'

'The babies died?'

'Everyone was killed there. They were made to breathe poison gas and that killed them.'

'Didn't any of them know what was happening? Why did they let themselves be taken to those camps?'

'They were taken by Hitler's army. The Nazis, the SS men. If they didn't do as they were told they were shot. They were pushed into cattle trucks on the railway as if they were animals and taken miles out into the country to be killed.'

'Mum? Don't cry!'

'No, it's stupid. So long ago.'

Lisa didn't feel like crying, she felt something much stranger. A shock, a shaking up of everything she knew. It was as if she lived in one of those snowstorm paperweights and had got used to the way the world around her looked while the glass dome was standing still. Now, suddenly, it had been shaken and nothing remained in its place.

'Did Hitler kill all the Jews?'

'Six million of them.' Lisa couldn't imagine six million of anything. She said, 'Was that what happened to Grandpa's mother and father?'

'Yes. And his little sister.'

'In one of those prisons? Was it poison gas?'

'I don't know exactly. John knows that they were taken to one of the camps and they never came out again. One of his mother's friends was there too and at the end of the war she was found, still alive, by the Allied soldiers. She told John about his family all being dead.'

'Why didn't Grandpa get killed too?'

'He very nearly was. He was meant to be going back to Vienna for the summer after he'd been in London, staying with a friend, but for some reason he didn't, he stayed on. The rest of the family obviously didn't think they were in any danger just then, although Hitler had started getting rid of the Jews in Germany before that.'

'So if Grandpa had gone back he'd have been killed too?'

'Almost certainly, he would.'

'Then Grandma couldn't have married him, and they wouldn't have had you, and you wouldn't have had me. I wouldn't be here.'

'Perhaps you'd have found someone else to be your Mum,' Fanny said.

'I wouldn't have liked that.'

'Silly! You'd have been her baby, and you wouldn't have known you could be anyone else.'

'That's funny!'

'What's funny?'

'Thinking about how I might have been someone else. Or I might never have got born at all.'

'Confusing,' Fanny said.

'Mum?'

'What now?'

'What was it that really stopped Grandpa going back to Vienna?'

'I'm not sure. John's never exactly told me. Lisa, I must go and do some work.'

'Wait a minute. There's something else . . .'

'What? Hurry up, love.'

But Lisa couldn't ask, in a hurry, whether her mother believed in ghosts, nor if she herself seemed to be going mad. She said, 'It doesn't matter. Go on, Mum. I'll do the washing up.'

The conversation had reminded her of something else. She had remembered the book she'd picked up months ago, *The Diary of Anne Frank*. She hadn't got beyond the first page, which had seemed boring, ordinary. But now she remembered something she'd been told. Anne Frank. Wasn't it about Hitler's war? And hadn't Anne Frank been Jewish?

She spent the rest of the afternoon reading. So it hadn't been only in Germany and Austria. In Holland, France, Hungary and in all the other countries that Hitler had conquered, his army had gone around killing Jews. Babies were killed, and girls like Anne Frank. If Lisa had been alive there then, she would have been killed too. It was extraordinary how knowing about one particular person to whom horrible things had happened made it all seem so much more real. You were told, 'Six million Jews were killed in the concentration camps' and it wasn't anything except a number. But if you read about Anne Frank and her family, you began to understand.

'It could have been me,' Lisa thought. But that didn't make it real. When there wasn't a war and it wasn't a crime to be Jewish, how could she, living in London, today, properly understand that sort of danger? When you couldn't go out into the street in case Hitler's soldiers found you? When you had to trust your friends to hide you, knowing that this would put them in danger too. That was what Grandpa had meant when he'd said that grown people could be afraid. He had said that they could be frightened of their neighbours, even of their friends. Perhaps he had been thinking of his own family, perhaps people they had loved and trusted had taught them that even friends can betray.

15

Things were better when the school term started and from having had too much time to herself, Lisa now had too little. She hadn't ever before been given so much work to take home; it kept her busy till supper time and often later in the evening as well. Weekends were also busy; Lisa noticed that her mother and Laurent were organizing outings for all five of them together, and she went along with this, partly because she didn't think excuses would be accepted, but mostly because she didn't want to be left alone at home. Although she would not admit it even to herself, she was becoming accustomed to having Pierre and Alice around. Sometimes she caught herself almost liking Pierre; he was certainly very quick, and could be witty. Once or twice she thought that she would have liked him to talk to her in the affectionate, teasing way he used towards Fanny. She remembered that long ago she had wished that she had an older brother, had thought it would be interesting and fun. She didn't feel at all like that about Alice, but she had reached the point where she was able to ignore her. In front of the adults, all three children would address each other when necessary, but it was with the fewest possible words.

The days passed, and life was normal. Nothing happened that couldn't be explained in the most ordinary way. But Lisa was always uneasily conscious that she had had an experience which she didn't understand. She tried to test herself in different ways. 'If I don't talk to myself when I'm alone, I can't be going mad.' 'If I don't have nightmares, I'm not going mad.' 'People who are really going mad never know about it, they always think they're sane and everyone else is mad.' But that wasn't much consolation; the saner she could prove herself to be, the madder she might really become. 'But my school work is all right and no one at home thinks I'm bonkers. A lot of people think they may have seen a ghost. Grandpa thinks he may have seen one, even Grandma isn't absolutely sure she hasn't.' That was a great reassurance. Grandma was certainly nowhere near being mad.

For the experiment which was to prove to herself that she was as sane as the next person, Lisa chose a bright morning, when the sun was illuminating her mother's bedroom. She had pleaded work to be finished when the others were going out for the usual Saturday morning shopping. She wanted to be alone in the house. It would be embarrassing to be found in front of her mother's long mirror, trying to see – or rather, not to see – a ghost.

No. The long mirror reflected only what she should see; shafts of dust-filled sunlight lying in tilted rays across the room. Lisa picked up the hand mirror. That too reflected the empty room. She turned round so that now it showed her the long mirror behind her. At first she thought she had succeeded, that there was nothing to be seen except herself against the sunny background. But she had been mistaken. It wasn't her mother's room which was reflected in the long mirror.

She was relieved to see that this time it wasn't the room she had seen before, but much lighter and longer. At first it seemed to Lisa quite unfamiliar, but as she looked round it, she realized that though the room was strange to her, the furniture was not. There was the long table with the same embroidered runner, and against a wall stood the tall, black cabinet with its shelf of photographs. At the far end were French windows leading out into a garden. She could see grass and the leaves of dark evergreen bushes.

She stepped forward, still looking into the hand mirror.

[83]

That only distanced the strange room. She stepped back-wards and knew that again she had gone through the mirror door and that when she turned round she would be in that other place and that other time. She walked to the open French window and looked out at the garden beyond. Immediately outside the window was a small patch of short grass, surrounded by thick laurel or rhododendron bushes, and standing perhaps ten feet away, in front of the bushes, was a boy. He looked curiously old-fashioned, like an illustration in an old children's book, with a thick tweed jacket above knickerbockers made of the same material. The knickerbockers ended tightly just below the knee.

He had dark curling hair cut very short, and dark eyes under black brows. He looked at Lisa as if she had taken him by surprise. He said, 'Hullo!' and at that moment a strange small girl came running through the bushes and said, 'Hans! I couldn't get Mummy to let me . . .' She stopped when she saw Lisa and she stared too. Then she said to the boy, 'Who's that?'

'I don't know. Who are you?' the boy asked Lisa.

She couldn't answer. She was confused. She had no idea who these children were, nor where she was or when.

'What are you doing here? Do you come from one of the other Square houses?' the boy was asking.

Lisa shook her head. But the words 'Square houses' reminded her of her grandmother's speaking of the Square garden and her misunderstanding of what that meant. She thought, 'This is the Square garden.'

'Why don't you say something?' the little girl asked.

Lisa opened her mouth, but nothing came out. Both children were waiting, staring.

'I don't believe he belongs here. I've never seen him before,' the girl said to the boy. To Lisa, she said, 'Which house have you come from?'

'He is probably just visiting,' the boy said. He spoke with a foreign accent.

'Perhaps he's dumb,' the girl said.

'Or he doesn't understand English,' the boy said. He asked a question then in a language Lisa had heard before. She shook her head.

'He doesn't speak German either,' the boy said.

And suddenly, Lisa understood. This was the boy her grandfather had been. She was with him, in the Square garden where he and Grandma had played together, and the time was Then. The time before the war. The time when little John – only he'd been called Hans then – was going back to Austria where he would be put into a prison camp and killed because he was Jewish. He didn't know that, but she did. She was the person who could warn him about the future.

She said, 'You're John – You're Hans Rosen. I've come to tell you . . . I've come to warn you . . .'

'Warn us about what?'

'About not going back to Vienna.'

'Why should I not go back to Vienna? It is my home,' the boy said.

Lisa didn't know how to answer. It was all too stupid. What she said to this boy could not possibly make any difference to her grandfather. He was safe, in her own time, in his house in the country. She knew that he hadn't been killed by the Nazis, he'd survived to marry and have a daughter, who was her own mother. So what could she say?

But suppose the way time worked wasn't like it seemed to be? Suppose what she did or didn't do really could make a difference to what happened? She took a deep breath. If none of this was real, if she was living in a hallucination, it didn't matter how much she made a fool of herself. She said to the boy, 'You mustn't go back there. It isn't safe for you. They might kill you.'

'Who would kill me?' the boy asked, and at the same time, the little girl said, 'Don't be silly. He's just trying to frighten you. He's horrible.'

'Who's he?' Lisa wondered, but she said, as firmly as she could, 'You should be frightened.'

'He's making it up. Don't listen to him,' the girl said to the boy.

'I'm not making it up! They're all going to die, and you will too, if you go back!' Lisa cried out because they wouldn't listen. She was angry now. 'I'm telling you, I know. There's going to be a war. If you go back, you'll get killed like everyone else. You have to stay in England. You mustn't ever go back!'

'If a war comes, I should be in my own country. I am Austrian,' the boy said.

'But you're Jewish,' Lisa said.

'What difference should that make?' the boy asked.

She didn't know how to tell him. What Fanny had told her had been in the past, over and done with, beyond repair. How could she tell this boy what was going to happen to him and his family and the millions of other families like them? She said, 'Hitler's going to kill all the Jews.'

'Hitler is in Germany. He has nothing to do with Austria. In Austria we wouldn't allow him to do this,' the boy said.

'He will be in Austria. He's going to have all the Jews taken away in cattle trucks and killed with poison gas.' She had not meant to blurt it out like this, but she felt the need to shock him into listening to her.

'This is nonsense. How can you know such things?'

'I do know! Everyone in your family is going to die. You will too, if you go back!' Lisa cried out to this unbelieving boy. She had forgotten for the moment that this was her grandfather sixty years ago. She felt that if she couldn't convince him of his danger, he would be killed.

'Is he mad, Hans? Come away, I don't like him,' the little girl was saying, and the boy turned to her and said, 'We should go in, I think. Don't worry, Evvie, my father says . . .' They were walking quickly away from her, and Lisa could not hear any more.

'Come back! It's true. I know!' Lisa cried out, and the sound of her voice was strange. It echoed as it should not have echoed among the shrubs, out of doors, but as if she was in a room.

She was in a room. She was walking away from Fanny's dressing table. She should have felt nothing but relief at escaping from the sooty garden and the two children who didn't believe her; but she could not escape from the feeling that she had made a fool of herself and that she had failed. She half expected to hear someone come running up the stairs to find out why she had cried out. But there were no feet on the stairs, no one opened the door of her mother's room. She left, and went to her own. It was terrible that she couldn't be alone there. Bloody Alice would soon be on the other side of the curtain again.

16

'It doesn't make sense. I know that Grandpa is alive and safe, so I know that he didn't go back to Vienna and get killed. There's no point in my trying to warn him about anything. He wouldn't believe me, anyway. That stupid little girl wouldn't let him, even if he wanted to.' These were Lisa's thoughts.

Her thoughts were very convincing. Then why didn't she feel certain that there was nothing else she ought to be doing? Why couldn't she simply dismiss the idea of going back into what she thought of as Elsbet's time, and stay where she was without worrying?

She was disturbed enough to want her mother to reassure her. In this house, which was now so full of people, it was difficult to find Fanny alone. At last, Lisa risked being told to go away and not to interrupt, and opened the door of what was now her mother's workroom.

'Yes? Lisa? What is it?'

'Can I come in for a minute, Mum?'

'I suppose so.' Not very promising. But then Fanny said, 'Sorry, love, I'm in the middle of something. But I won't be long. Or, tell you what! I need a model. Could you sit over there and read a book, or pretend to, for five minutes? And if you could look as if you were cross about something, sulking a bit, that'd be really great.'

Lisa sat over there and read one of her mother's magazines and, without much trouble, looked cross. She'd often modelled for her mother before, and she knew that the most important part of the exercise was to keep still.

It was more than five minutes. One of her arms had gone to sleep and she was feeling that she couldn't keep the pose any longer, when Fanny said, 'You aren't looking cross, you're looking worried. Never mind. I'll turn your mouth down at the corners and put in a frown, that'll do the trick. All right, that's it! Thanks, love. I wish it was a better book that you're going to be immortalized in.'

Lisa stretched. She watched her mother tidying away pens and pencils and colours and paper and thought it wasn't surprising if she looked worried rather than cross. She tried to think how she could broach the subject which was occupying her mind.

'Mum!'

'What, love?'

'Can you explain how time works?'

'What an extraordinary question? What's put you on to that?'

'I just wondered if it's really the way it seems.'

'How does it seem? To you?'

Lisa found this difficult to answer. 'I suppose knowing that one day starts after the last one has finished. And things happening after each other.'

'I'd agree. That's how time seems to me, too.'

'Could it be different? Could something we do now make a difference to something that happened a long time ago?'

'I don't see how. If it really happened years ago, nothing we do today is going to change it, is it?'

This was what she'd wanted to hear. 'It couldn't, could it?'

'Not unless you're one of the people who believe that there's no such thing as time.'

'How can they? Of course there's time,' Lisa said.

'But it may not be how we think it is. One thing happening after another. It could depend on how you looked at it.'

'But things do happen after each other. Don't they?'

'We think they do. But it could be like looking in a mirror,

and seeing things the other way round. Back to front. Or . . .
I know what it's like. You know how when you're sitting in
a bus, you can see reflections in the windows of what's
outside? But the reflection isn't where it should be. I mean,
you see things that look as if they're behind you and then
suddenly you see that instead, they're in front, just coming
up.'

'Ye-es. I know what you mean.'

'Well, suppose time's like that. We think we can see it all
happening neatly, this thing coming after that, and then the
next one and so on, but really they're not in that order at all.
They may not have an order. They may all be going on at the
same time, only we can't see that, and we arrange what we
think we see so that it fits in with what we believe.'

'I'm not sure I understand,' Lisa said.

'I'm not surprised. I don't understand it myself well
enough to explain it properly. Why are you asking about
time, anyway?'

She couldn't say. Ghosts? Finding herself back in a time
when Grandpa was a young boy? She said, 'I was just
thinking.'

'What's all this about? Have you got to write a com-
position on time, or something like that?' Fanny asked.

No. It wasn't as simple as a school exercise. Lisa knew
that she had to decide whether she believed in what she'd
seen in the double mirror image, or if she could convince
herself that she need not feel any anxiety for the young
Jewish boy in London years ago. But she knew one thing.
She passionately did not want to go back in time again.

17

Time.

If time wasn't as it seemed. If what you did today didn't lead on to what happened tomorrow, then everything was so muddled and mysterious, you couldn't be sure of anything.

Sometimes she decided that she was going to forget the whole business. It didn't make sense. She must have been crazy to believe that what she did now and here could possibly make any difference to Grandpa or what had happened to him in the last war.

But she couldn't forget completely. It was possible when she was at school, surrounded by friends, in lessons, during games. But at other times the niggling doubt came back. She found herself sitting over her homework with her mind far away. She might take an hour to work out one equation which should have taken fifteen minutes. Sometimes her eyes followed the lines of the book on French history, and when she turned the page she realized that although she had faithfully 'read' every word of every sentence, she hadn't taken in the sense at all. She might as well have been sitting in front of a blank sheet of paper. Instead of absorbing the events leading up to the French revolution, she had been wondering what would happen – what would actually *happen* – if she did what she wanted. Which was nothing.

Grandpa couldn't suddenly disappear. And if he did disappear now, because he'd been murdered in a Nazi death camp fifty years ago, then where would Fanny be? Would she disappear too? Which would mean that Lisa herself wouldn't ever have existed. Then she wondered if there might be another family who might have survived Hitler's war, but had not because no one had warned them to escape, and if there was another Lisa somewhere else who had never managed to get born because of this. A sort of ghost child, waiting in limbo for parents who were already dead.

It was not cold in January, but at the beginning of February the temperature suddenly dropped. Each morning the roofs of the houses were glistening white with frost, and the wind from the east was bitter. Then for half a day it was warmer and that night there was a steady snowfall. At first London looked white and strange and beautiful, but before the evening the pavements were covered with dirty brown slush, which froze during the night, so that in the morning people were slipping and falling. Drivers on the motorway drove too fast and there were multiple pileups and accidents. Pipes in houses froze, standby pipes appeared in the streets, railway signals went out of action, trains were cancelled. Lisa heard Pierre say to Fanny, 'Why is everything suddenly not working? Have you not had snow here before?'

'We have it quite often, but we never seem ready for it. It's the same when there's a long dry summer, we run out of water, and everyone's surprised.'

'It is not . . . clever.'

Fanny agreed. She seemed amused, but Lisa was cross. 'If you don't like it, you don't have to stay,' she wanted to say. The annoying thing was that Pierre's criticism was true, she'd thought it herself. And she hated the cold. It bit into her bones and she found it difficult to think. The only advantage was that while she was fighting to keep warm, she almost managed to forget her problems. It was as if the whole affair had gone into the freezer; but she knew, at the back of her mind, that it was there, and that she hadn't decided what to do about it.

The cold spell ended as suddenly as it had begun. Now the pipes that had frozen dripped water through ceilings and down walls. There were no plumbers to be had, the thaw brought as much trouble as the freeze-up. Halfway through February, Fanny said to Lisa, 'Laurent's got to go to Italy for a few days on business. He's arranged for it to be while you're off school for the half term week, so that I can go with him and you can go and stay with Grandma and Grandpa. All right?'

Lisa said, 'I suppose so,' which sounded less enthusiastic than she really felt. She looked forward to staying with her grandparents again and being the only child around, a little spoiled, getting away from Pierre and, especially, Alice.

'Pierre and Alice will be going too,' Fanny said.

'You mean, with you?'

'How can we take them on a business trip? They'll go with you.'

'To Grandma's?'

'That's right.'

'Then I won't go.'

'Lisa, be sensible. You can't stay here on your own.'

'I could. I'd be quite all right.'

'I wouldn't be. You know I can't go away and leave you here alone.'

'I don't see why not,' Lisa said.

'Well, I'm not going to.'

'Why can't they go somewhere else? Why do they have to go to Grandma's?'

'There isn't anywhere else for them to go.'

Lisa knew it was no good suggesting that they should go to their mother. 'Haven't they got relations or friends or someone in France?'

'Not that they could get to easily. Anyway, Grandpa wants to have them.'

'Will I have to share a room with Alice again?'

'I don't know. Grandma will decide that.'

'I'm not going if she puts Alice in with me.'

'Lisa, please don't be difficult. I'm certainly not going to leave you here by yourself. You generally like going to stay with Grandma.'

'Not with Alice, I don't.'

'There isn't any other way we can manage. I suppose you aren't suggesting that I should stay here with you instead of going to Italy?'

Lisa couldn't say that this was what she had meant. She said nothing.

'Don't let's have any more arguments. You've got to go,' Fanny said, and left the room.

Two days later, Lisa was surprised when Laurent stopped her on the stairs.

'Will you come with me for five minutes, Lisa? I want to talk to you.'

Expecting trouble, she followed him into the kitchen.

'Sit down,' he said and placed himself opposite her at the table.

'Fanny tells me that you are saying you don't want to stay with your grandparents next week,' he said.

Lisa didn't answer.

'Is that right? You are saying you won't go?'

'I don't want to.'

'Do you know that Fanny is wondering if she should stay here with you, instead of coming to Rome with me?'

'She didn't say that.'

'She is saying it now. But I am not listening to her. I am not going to let her stay here with you just because you don't want to go to Lorrimer. I will not let her sacrifice herself . . . and me.'

'She doesn't have to stay here. I can stay by myself.'

'You know she won't allow that. She would worry all the time, if she knew you were here alone.'

'That's stupid. I'm quite old enough,' Lisa said.

'I don't know if you are or not, but if Fanny thinks you are not, she will not leave you here. And I am not going away without her, so you must make up your mind to do what has been arranged.'

He had never spoken to her like this before. It had always been her mother who had said, 'You must do this' or 'You can't do that'. Lisa hadn't quite the courage to say, 'You aren't my father, I don't have to do what you tell me.' Instead, she hunched her shoulders and muttered.

'What are you saying?'

'Nothing.'

'That is good, because I have several things I am going to say to you.' He stopped. Lisa looked down at the table. She didn't want to listen to what he was going to say, and if she looked at Laurent's face, she would have to.

'I think it is not easy for you, to have a new father and a brother and sister living in this house. I have felt sorry for you. At first I thought "It is natural that Lisa should be disturbed when she has been accustomed to being all alone with Fanny," and I told Pierre and Alice to be patient and to understand if you did not try to be friendly with them at once. But now I am beginning not to feel sorry any more. It appears to me that you don't make any effort with my children. They don't tell me anything, but I can see that you behave as if they were still strangers in this house. Of course this isn't agreeable for them, and it can't be agreeable for you either. You are behaving as if you think that if you make yourself disagreeable enough, we are all going to go away for ever. I want to tell you now that we are not going away, and that the person you are hurting most by being like this, is yourself. You hurt your mother, too, but it is you who will suffer most at last.'

Lisa still wouldn't look at him. If she could have closed the ears of her understanding against him, she would have done so.

'So I am telling you now. You will go to Lorrimer while we are away, and I should advise you to be polite to my children, even if you can't be friendly. I think your grandfather would not be pleased if he knew how you feel about them.'

'You can't make me go,' Lisa said.

'You will go, and you will try to behave,' Laurent said. He got up and went out of the kitchen.

She had to swallow the tears of furious resentment until she could be alone. There were voices in the hall, and in her own bedroom she would know that horrible Alice was on the other side of the curtain, listening. She made a quick dash to the only place where she could be sure of not being disturbed. She locked herself into the bathroom, sat on the closed lavatory seat, and choked with anger. She wanted to scream and allow herself to sob, but even here she had to be careful not to make more noise than would be drowned by the swish of the water in the pan when she flushed the lavatory.

18

At Lorrimer, Lisa was aware that while her grandfather treated all three children the same, this was not true of her grandmother. Grandpa summoned them for walks or for jobs to be done about the house and garden, and seemed equally pleased to be with any one of the three. Grandma, however, always said which child she wanted, and Lisa knew that she was singled out for the more interesting tasks. But she saw that Grandma liked Pierre; they had long conversations, when it was Pierre's duty to correct Grandma's halting French and to supply the words she didn't know. To Lisa's satisfaction, she realized that Grandma did not much care for Alice, who was treated with an over scrupulous politeness. It wasn't surprising that Alice attached herself to Grandpa. 'It isn't fair! They're my relations, not hers! I'm left out!' Lisa raged inside herself, while outwardly she had to be polite and even appear to be friendly.

At least she and Alice did not have to share a bedroom here; Grandma had put Lisa in the best spare room, where Fanny and Laurent had slept at Christmas. But even this had its sting; Alice was in the little spare room, which had always been Lisa's, and Pierre, on the sofa bed in the living room, couldn't go to sleep until Grandma and Grandpa were ready to go to bed, which gave him almost grown-up status. Though Grandpa had taken to going to bed much earlier than had been usual with him, and Lisa noticed that, as her mother had said, he was very pale and became tired after quite short walks. She wondered if there was really something wrong with him, or if it was just his age. He often said how much he disliked the winter. Probably like weeding, it made him feel a hundred years old.

'You are making life very hard for yourself,' Grandpa surprisingly said to her one morning when he and she were walking in the wood to collect kindling and to look for snowdrops.

'What d'you mean?'

'You are fighting against your family.'

'They're not my family!' Lisa said, and then regretted understanding too quickly.

'Alice and Pierre are your family now. Listen, Lisa. It is no use to look all the time for things to dislike . . . to hate. If you look, you can always find these things. About anyone, even the people you love best . . .'

'No, I wouldn't! I don't hate anything about you.'

'You hate that I like to talk to Pierre and Alice. You are angry with me for that.'

'I'm not exactly angry,' Lisa said.

'Something like being angry. What I have to say to you is that if you allow yourself to be hating all the time, it is you who will become hateful.'

'I don't see . . .'

'I am not going to tell you what is good about your brother and sister. You will have to find that out for yourself. But I must tell you to stop this war with them.'

'It isn't a war.'

'The feeling is like a war. I am telling you this because I love you, Lisa, and I don't want to see you spoil your life.'

She was embarrassed. No one except Grandpa would have said it straight out like that, 'I love you.' But she liked it, too. She wished she could say back, 'And I love you,' but she couldn't. She didn't say anything. He said, 'Look! My first crocuses. They have never been so late as this year,' and the conversation was over. Afterwards when she thought about it, she tried to believe that he had exaggerated. She wasn't conducting a war against Pierre and Alice, she just didn't like them. But several times she heard his words in her ears: 'It is you who will become hateful' and, what she would much rather remember: 'I love you, Lisa.'

At the end of the week Fanny and Laurent came to fetch them back to London. They'd brought presents for everyone, a striped Roman scarf for Grandma, a bottle of Strega for Grandpa, silky shirts of different colours for Lisa, Pierre and Alice. They had had a wonderful time, it had been warm, they'd sat in the sun and they'd seen beautiful places and things. 'Your holiday has done you good. You should take her away more often,' Grandpa said to Laurent.

'I would like it, but it is not always easy to arrange,' Laurent said. Did he look at Lisa, as he said it? Or had she imagined it? That night, before she went up to bed, Lisa was caught for a moment by her mother. 'How did things go at Lorrimer?'

'All right.' She wasn't going to admit that it hadn't been as bad as she'd expected.

'Grandma said they'd enjoyed having you.'

Lisa wouldn't answer that. She didn't know if 'you' meant just her or the other two as well.

That night she dreamed about Elsbet. She was in a garden, searching for something that her grandfather wanted and which she couldn't find. The garden was strange; the lawn and the roses were like those in her grandparents' garden, but there were also dark shrubs and twisting gravel paths like a park in the city. Lisa was looking everywhere without being sure what she was looking for. She kept on finding things, a garden tool, a book, the Roman scarf, but she knew, each time, that this was not the object of her search. Then, standing outside the garden, on the further side of the beech hedge, she saw the child, Elsbet. Lisa said, 'What are you doing there? Why don't you come in? I've been looking for you.' But Elsbet didn't reply. She stood without moving, a stone girl without a voice. 'Why don't you come in?' Lisa asked again, annoyed, but Elsbet still didn't answer, nor did she move. Only looking closely at her, Lisa saw tears running down her cheeks. 'It isn't that she's a real girl crying, she's a statue, it's rain that looks like tears,' Lisa said to herself. So there was nothing that she ought to do to try to comfort Elsbet or to bring her within the garden. But as she looked around her, she saw that the sun was shining. So how could it be raining too? She said, loudly, 'It's raining. I know it's raining.'

A voice said '*Pardon*?'

Lisa woke. She was in bed at home. No garden, no Elsbet, no rain. The voice from the other side of the curtain said again, '*Pardon*?'

'Nothing. I didn't say anything.'

'I heard you speak. About the rain,' Alice said.

'No, I didn't. You must have been dreaming.'

No answer. It took time for Lisa to get back to sleep.

19

It was two days later, that Lisa suddenly had a new idea.

'Mum!'

'What, Lisa?'

'Elsbet. Grandpa's little sister. Is Grandpa quite sure . . .?'

'What on earth made you think of her?' Fanny asked.

'I've seen photographs of her. Grandma showed me. You said she was killed in one of those camps.'

'That's what Grandpa was told.'

'Couldn't she possibly have escaped, somehow?'

'I should think it's very unlikely.'

'Did that woman who told him about his mother and father say that Elsbet was dead too?'

'I imagine she did. I don't think there's ever been any question about it in Dad's mind. He did go back to Austria after the war to see if he could find out anything about his family, but there was nothing. I told you, all that was left in the apartment they'd lived in was my big mirror.'

Lisa did not want to think about the mirror. She said, 'I don't see how anyone can be sure.'

'I wish you wouldn't go on about it, Lisa. It's over. And don't ask Grandpa about her, will you? I know he's always felt bad that he was the only one of his family to escape. You don't want to upset him.'

But was it over? Why did Lisa feel as if it was happening now? She thought, 'If I went back again I could try to make Elsbet believe me this time, perhaps she'd escape from Hitler too. Then Grandpa wouldn't have to feel bad about her. She might really be alive somewhere he's never thought of.'

She had read about long lost relatives turning up. She'd seen a programme on television about two old sisters each of whom had thought the other was dead. She had seen them meeting at an airport, looking into each other's wrinkled faces and crying. If she could bring Elsbet back, as if from the dead, Grandpa would be pleased. He wouldn't say, 'You will become hateful.' He would say to Elsbet, 'I love you,' as he'd said to Lisa, and he would love Lisa even better for having saved his sister.

It made sense. She would save Elsbet. She would go back. She felt heroically brave.

She had to choose her time when there was no one else in the house. It was important not to be interrupted. All she had to do was to pretend that she didn't want to go to the cinema with the others, and she would have the house to herself. At the end of a wet Saturday afternoon, when Laurent and Fanny had taken Pierre and Alice to a French film (which Lisa would rather have liked to see, so that refusing made her feel all the more noble and self-sacrificing), she sat in front of the Viennese mirror in her mother's room and picked up the hand mirror.

She turned her head to look into it, then she hesitated. She had remembered something. Grandpa's mother and father and Elsbet had been imprisoned because they were Jews. She, Lisa, was Jewish too. In that world, she was not invisible; Elsbet had seen her. She might not be able to reach the mirror to make her escape. She might be taken to one of those camps and executed like Anne Frank, like the rest of Grandpa's family. If she went back of her own accord, from her safe life here and now, to die there, she would be a sort of martyr. Little Saint Lisa. Was she brave enough to risk that? 'I can't go back. It's dangerous. And anyway I probably wouldn't be able to do anything to help,' she thought.

She remembered then that the last time she had stepped through the mirror, she had found herself in the London house, where Elsbet too had lived. It wouldn't be dangerous to go there. She would try.

But when she looked into the hand mirror, she saw, in the big mirror behind her, the room with dark furniture and framed photographs, and she was overtaken by panic. She put the hand mirror back on Fanny's dressing table. 'Nothing I could do Now would make any difference to Then,' she said, half aloud, and hoped that it was true.

She was restless and miserable for the rest of the afternoon. Nothing seemed worth doing. She wished she had gone to the cinema with the others. It was annoying to hear that it had been a fantastic film which they knew she'd have enjoyed. When Fanny asked how she had been doing, Lisa couldn't think of any reasonable answer. She said, 'I did some homework,' which was true, but sounded false.

She wanted to forget. It wasn't fair that she should be in this position. No one else of her age cared about the Hitler war, it was all far too long ago. She might as well be troubled about what had happened at Waterloo, or the Battle of Trafalgar. Or Agincourt, or a war in ancient Greece.

Lisa felt as if she was being split in two. She was angry and she was hurt, and at the same time she felt guilty, and her guilt made her even more furious. Furious with Fanny for bringing these obnoxious strangers to share their life, furious with the two strangers for being there; and most of all furious with herself for not being able to make up her mind to dare to go into the dangerous past.

In a brief moment the following week when she found herself alone with Fanny, she asked, 'Mum! Do you think I'm a brave person?'

Fanny thought for a moment before she said, 'What sort of brave? Do you mean not minding having an injection or going to the dentist? You've always been good at that sort of thing. I don't know about the other sort of courage. You haven't ever been asked to risk your life for someone else's, have you?'

Lisa wished she could say, 'That's what I'm having to decide about now.' But she couldn't. She said, 'Suppose I knew there was someone asleep in a burning house, do you think I'd go in to save them?'

'I've no idea. Do you think you would?'

'While we're talking about it like this, I think I would. But if it really happened, I don't know. Would you, Mum?'

'I don't know, either. So if you're a coward, so am I, probably.'

'Do you know anyone who did risk her life to save someone?'

'Someone I knew once, tried to rescue a boy who couldn't swim in a very rough sea. But he couldn't. They both drowned.'

'So it wasn't any good him trying?'

'I wouldn't say that. I've always thought that even if you knew you were taking quite a big risk, you'd have to do it because of what you'd feel like afterwards if you hadn't tried. Of course if you knew for certain that it was hopeless you wouldn't feel so bad.'

It was hopeless. Grandpa was alive and well and Elsbet was dead and nothing she did was going to change these facts. But Lisa wished she was quite certain in her mind about this.

20

'I don't want to go back to Vienna. It can't make any difference whether I do or not. I don't have to do anything,' Lisa thought.

She was uncomfortable. She couldn't make herself concentrate. She was getting poor marks for her school work. 'I don't know what's come over you since half term. This last piece of work is disgraceful, a child of six wouldn't have made such stupid mistakes. If you don't do better before the end of term you'll have to go down to the lower division for maths,' Mrs Lansdowne said. Mrs Lansdowne was strict, but fair and Lisa liked her a lot.

'It was difficult,' Lisa said.

'Nonsense. You've tackled far more difficult problems before and found you could cope. Don't hand in work like this again,' Mrs Lansdowne said.

'I'm sorry.'

'Is anything troubling you at home? No one in your family is ill? You can tell me if there's a reason for your work suddenly going downhill like this, you know.'

Lisa longed to say how she felt. But it wasn't possible to explain to anyone, least of all her maths teacher, that she couldn't decide whether she ought to go back fifty years in time in order to try to save a great aunt she had never seen. It didn't make sense. So she said politely that, No, thank you, there was nothing wrong at home and she'd try to do better.

Suddenly the weather changed. The wind was coming from the south, there were daffodils on the big grassy bank on the hill leading up to the common, little pointed leaf buds on bushes. As Lisa walked to school, she heard birds warning off intruders with delicious trills and arpeggios. The mornings and evenings were lighter. People turned down the collars of their thick coats and left their woolly scarves at home. Lisa noticed all these changes and wished that she felt happier and lighter, as everyone else seemed to do. She didn't. She felt weighed down with the need to come to some decision, and however much she tried to persuade herself that nothing she did could possibly make any difference to what had happened nearly fifty years ago, she still couldn't forget it.

'Are we going away for Easter?' she asked Fanny one day near the end of the spring term.

'I'm not sure if we'll be able to. I've got this big job to finish and the publishers are in a hurry. They always are in a hurry. It's a pity they don't pay extra for rushed work,' Fanny said.

'I could go and stay with Grandma,' Lisa said.

'If you do, the others will have to go too, and I'm not sure whether I should ask them to put up with three of you. John hasn't been very well.'

'What's wrong with him?' Lisa asked.

'They haven't found out yet. He's been going to the hospital for tests, and they said he might have to go as an in-patient.'

'Is he badly ill? Has he got cancer? He's not going to die?' Lisa was frightened. She couldn't imagine Grandpa not being there.

'They haven't discovered yet what's wrong. No one has said anything about cancer. I don't know what they suspect.'

Lisa noticed now that when she wasn't laughing, her mother looked different. She was thinner, there were lines on her face which hadn't been there in the winter. She said, 'Mum? Are you worried about Grandpa?'

'Of course I'm worried. I'm worried about both of them.

I think John's had a lot of pain and he's not sleeping well, and my mother's anxious about him. Naturally. They're neither of them exactly young. They're both over sixty, you know.'

'Sixty's not terribly old, is it? Lots of people live till they're eighty or ninety or something.'

'Let's hope they will,' Fanny said.

'Mum! Can't I go to Lorrimer by myself? Just for a little?'

'I don't really want to ask my mother just now, Lisa. Wait till the result of these last tests comes through. If it's good and my father feels better, I daresay you could go down for a night or two.'

There was no news about Lisa's grandfather for the next three days. Then, one evening, Fanny had a long conversation on the telephone and came back into the kitchen in tears.

'Fanny! It is your father . . .?' Laurent said, jumping up from the table and putting an arm round her.

'He's had to go into hospital. They're going to operate.'

'What . . .? Has anyone been told what is wrong?'

'Not exactly. They say it's exploratory.'

'But that needn't mean anything.'

'Mum says that everyone's being so bloody reassuring, she's sure they think it's something really bad.'

'Sit down and finish your supper. You will want to go to Lorrimer tomorrow.'

'Tonight.'

'My dearest, if you set off now, at once, you would not reach your mother's house till midnight. Then she has to wait up for you, and there is nothing you can do. Go tomorrow morning. Then, when your father is in hospital, you will be there to comfort her. There would be less . . . bother? Fussage?'

'Fuss,' Fanny said, with what was almost a smile.

'Fuss. You can make your own bed, cook for yourself. Your mother would have to do all those things for you if you arrive suddenly in the night. Really, you should not go till tomorrow.'

So it was early the next morning that Fanny drove off. She looked as if she hadn't slept all night. She kissed Pierre and Alice and said, 'See you soon.' As she hugged Lisa, she said, 'I know you'll be anxious. I'll phone as soon as there's any news and . . .' Lisa knew what she wanted to say, and in spite of herself felt she had to help her. She said, 'Don't worry about me, Mum. I'm not going to fight anyone.'

'That's my good girl.' Fanny drove away, and the family left behind went back to their interrupted breakfasts.

She rang that evening. The operation was scheduled for the next day. She'd been to the hospital and seen John, who didn't look too bad and did not seem at all anxious. Her mother was the person who needed her now. 'She needs someone to talk to. Some of it is about being frightened now, but a lot is about things that happened when they were young together. It was a good thing I didn't rush off last night. Now I'll stay at any rate until the op's over. I'm glad I brought some work with me, we both need time on our own, Mum and me.'

The next day was horrible. Lisa couldn't think of anything except what was happening to Grandpa in the hospital. Were they cutting him open now? Where would they cut? What would they find? Was Fanny going to ring them up tonight to tell them that he had cancer or something as bad? Or, worse, would she have to say that he'd died 'without regaining consciousness', which was a phrase Lisa had heard before about people in hospital. By the end of the school day, she was almost too tired to feel anxious. Laurent was in the house when she got home but when she asked, 'Any news?' he shook his head.

'Is it bad that this operation is not yet finished?' Pierre asked.

Lisa almost said, 'I don't know why you should mind. He's not your grandfather.' But she remembered that she'd told Fanny that she wouldn't fight anyone, so she said nothing.

It was nine o'clock before Fanny telephoned. The good news was that the surgeons hadn't found anything terrible, there was no cancer, the operation had been successful. But John had been in the operating theatre for four hours, and he was not recovering as well as they had hoped. He was wired up to machines, he looked dreadful. The doctors were quite hopeful, but he wasn't out of danger. Fanny and her mother were going to spend the night in the hospital.

'He can't die! He escaped from Hitler, he can't die now!' Lisa thought.

No one spoke much that evening. It was a very silent supper. When Lisa said good night to Laurent, she had the impression that he wanted to say something kind, something comforting, but didn't know how. He took her hand, which he didn't usually do for good night, and held it for a moment. Then he said, 'Try to sleep, Lisa. There will be news in the morning.'

21

Lisa could not sleep.

She thought about Grandpa, lying in the hospital bed wired up to tubes and bottles like the people she'd seen on the television. She thought of his voice, saying, 'I am telling you this because I love you, Lisa.' A hot tear rolled down her cheek on to the pillow. He had said,' . . . If you allow yourself to be hating . . . it is you who will become hateful . . .' She thought about Alice and Pierre. She couldn't imagine that she would ever feel different about them. They were her enemies. They were her enemies just as Hitler and his SS men had been the enemies of her grandfather's family in Vienna. If she had said this to anyone else, she would have been told that it was ridiculous; how could a quarrel with others of her own age possibly be compared with what Hitler had done to the Jews?

She had to go to school the next day, tired already after a night of broken sleep. There had been no more news. 'Probably there has not been much change in John's condition. If anything bad had happened, Fanny would have let us know,' was all the comfort Laurent could give her. So it was another wasted day as far as school work was concerned. She was told that she was being lazy, uncooperative, difficult. But she felt too tired to mind. She didn't listen properly even to Mrs Lansdowne's scolding, and was surprised when it stopped suddenly and Mrs Lansdowne said, 'You're half asleep. What's wrong?'

'I didn't sleep properly last night.'

'Why not? Any special reason?'

This time it was possible to say, 'My grandfather's in hospital and we're all worried about him.'

'I'm sorry. I hope he gets better soon. All the same, you really must try to concentrate.'

When she got back from school that afternoon, the house felt horribly empty. Pierre and Alice always arrived home later than she did. And it was cold. In the warm spell a day or two before, Fanny had turned off the central heating and now an east wind had chilled every room in the house. Hot tea in the kitchen was good and Lisa sat over it, warming her hands on the mug. She knew why she didn't want to go upstairs to do her homework. She would not be able to pass her mother's room without glancing in to see the big mirror waiting, as if it had really been a door.

'Lisa, you're shivering! Are you feeling all right?' Laurent asked her at supper.

'I'm all right,' Lisa lied.

'You don't look well, and you've hardly eaten anything.'

'I'm just not hungry.'

It was another miserable evening and Lisa went to bed with that feeling of exhausted wakefulness which meant that again she wouldn't be able to get to sleep. When she closed her eyes she saw a boy and a girl in a garden, turning away because they thought she was mad. She saw a little girl in her best dress, trying to keep a straight face for the camera. She saw a wildly escaping kitten and she saw the blood springing from a child's wounded arm. Presently she heard Alice come into the room, preparing quietly behind the curtain, for bed. Lisa found that in spite of herself she wanted to call out, to hear Alice's voice, so that she could be certain she was back in today's safe ordinary life. But she lay still, and soon she could hear from the regular breathing on the other side of the curtain that Alice was asleep. She heard distant sounds of quiet steps on the stairs and the shutting of other bedroom doors. She thought of Fanny's bedroom and the long mirror. Lisa did not want to relive those dreams . . . hallucinations . . . whatever they were, but her mind would not leave them.

Elsbet had taken her for a boy. So had Hans and Evelyn. Why?

Of course! In the dark room in Vienna, in the London house with the Square garden, she had been wearing her ordinary clothes, jeans and a sweater. And her hair was almost as short as a boy's. It had been she, Lisa, who had walked through the mirror into a time long before she was born, when Grandpa and Grandma were children. She had been the boy ghost Grandma didn't want to talk about. It had been her warning that Grandpa had spoken of when he had said that only a ghost boy could have known of the terrible things that were to come. Had that played any part in persuading him to stay in England instead of returning to Austria? It was nonsense to believe this, and yet it made sense. And Elsbet? She didn't believe that she had succeeded in convincing Elsbet. Elsbet had not believed her, and Elsbet was dead.

She felt as if she had been lying awake for hours, when, instead of lying in bed and trying not to remember, she found that she was walking down a flight of unfamiliar stairs. It was half dark, she couldn't see the steps, she was guiding herself by her hand on the rounded banister. At the bottom of the stairs she could just see a square hallway, and through a door beyond open on to a road she could see the figures of people passing. She crossed the hall, went to the door and stepped out.

She was in a street of tall, dark stone houses, and the street was full of people. They were a mixed crowd; old men with beards, old women with shawls over their heads, younger men and women leading small children and carrying babies in their arms. They flowed past where she stood, not speaking, hardly looking at each other, walking slowly but never stopping, except that once an old woman fell to the ground. Hands were reached out to help her, and she was up and moving again; the incident hardly checked that relentless march. Lisa looked into some of the faces and what she saw was horrible. What was impelling these people to move along the street was not the wish to reach another place. It was terror. Something or someone was forcing them to walk, and they knew that the end of their journey was death.

Now she saw that there were groups of families clinging together as they marched, wives and husbands supporting each other, older children carrying the younger. A small girl passing near her, on the outskirts of the crowd, seemed to be alone. Lisa recognized her. She cried out, 'Elsbet!' At the sound of her voice, other children looked towards her and they were all Elsbet; twenty, fifty, a hundred Elsbets with tangled dark hair and big dark eyes. The child nearest to her, held out something for her to take, and Lisa saw that it was the kitten that the mirror image Elsbet had carried into the room of polished wood. Lisa drew back into the shelter of a high doorway, but the child came after her, urgently trying to make her take the little cat. Lisa knew that if she did, she would become another of those doomed people, she would have to walk with them along the silent street, she would share their fate. She cried out, 'No! I can't No!'

Her own voice woke her. For a moment, she didn't know where she was. Something was wrapped round her so that it was difficult to move her arms. She said, 'No!' out loud again before she discovered that it was her own bedclothes which were twisted round her as if she had fought with them. She was sweating, but she was cold. She was shivering with fear.

A voice from the other side of the curtain startled her. Alice said, 'Is something wrong?'

Lisa couldn't answer.

'I heard you calling,' Alice said. Lisa heard her get out of bed and heard the rattle of the curtain as it was pulled aside. 'Are you ill?' Alice asked.

'No,' Lisa said.

'Shall I fetch someone? I am sorry Fanny is not here.'

Lisa, still wrapped in the horror of her dream, felt her heart lurch. The real world wasn't any better than the nightmare city she had just left. It wasn't only Elsbet who had been walking towards the grave, Grandpa too was in danger, might already have died. Her throat was tight, hot tears rolled down her face. She tried to cry quietly, then perhaps Alice wouldn't notice. But before Alice had gone back to her side of the curtain, Lisa sobbed. Once she had started, she couldn't stop. She rolled over on to her front and tried to stifle the sound in her pillow.

'I will fetch Laurent,' she heard Alice say.

'No! I don't want . . .'

'You are ill?'

'No. I dreamed . . .' She was astonished when she felt a hand on her forehead, quickly withdrawn. Then she found that Alice was straightening out her bedclothes, releasing her from what had felt like cords round her chest. Alice's hand found hers and held it. Surprisingly, this was comforting. Lisa did not pull away.

'You are very sad. Is it about your grandfather? I am sad for him too,' Alice said.

'Grandpa!' Lisa said between more painful sobs.

'You are cold. Shall I fetch a blanket from my bed?'

She brought the blanket and spread it over Lisa, but Lisa still shivered. She felt as if she would never be warm again.

'Shall I go back now?' Alice was asking.

Lisa said, 'Don't go.' Something she had never thought she'd be saying to Alice.

'I am becoming cold too,' Alice said.

Lisa couldn't say the words to suggest that Alice come into her bed, but she moved nearer to the wall and held back the coverings to show what she meant. Also without speaking, Alice climbed in and lay beside her. It wasn't a big bed, they had to arrange themselves so that they fitted into it. Lisa rolled over to face the wall and felt Alice lying along her back. Alice's body was deliciously warm. Lisa's spine felt as if it was beginning to unlock, as if it had been frozen into hard splintery ice which was now melting. She put a cautious hand behind her and found Alice's. That was comforting too. Alice put an arm over her shoulders. Each of them curled a little, so that they lay like forks in a cutlery drawer, neatly fitting each other's curves. Alice was asleep almost at once, and minutes later Lisa too was warm and sleeping.

She woke in the bright morning with a start. She remembered first with astonishment, that Alice had come into her bed last night. She wasn't there now, and the room was entirely silent. Perhaps it had been a dream. Certainly the other hadn't been real, the nightmare. She didn't want to think about it, but it wouldn't go away. It had left her not only still frightened, but also guilty. She hadn't tried to do anything to help any of those marching people. She had refused to help Elsbet. Last, she remembered Grandpa, and felt guilty again. She had forgotten him. She felt bad that a dream about things that had happened so long ago could have wiped out her anxiety about his illness.

Her bedside clock said half past nine. It couldn't be as late as that! But the sun was high and she realized she was hungry. She got up and dressed and went downstairs.

In the kitchen she found Laurent.

'Alice told me you slept badly, so I didn't wake you. I will write a note for you to take to school this afternoon,' he said.

Lisa got herself her usual breakfast. Cereal, toast, tea. She was glad she hadn't got to face Alice just yet. Her feelings were chaotic. She didn't know if Alice was still an enemy or not. In a curious way she wanted to go on hating her. She didn't want to have to change.

The telephone bell rang sharply and made her jump. Laurent took up the receiver. He was saying, 'Yes. Yes. That's wonderful. I am so glad. Yes, I'll tell them. They have all been worried. You could speak to Lisa now, if you like. No, nothing bad, she just didn't sleep well last night. She'll be going this afternoon.' He gestured to Lisa and handed her the phone. She heard Fanny's voice. 'Lisa? It's good news. Grandpa's better. I'm at the hospital. They say he's going to be all right. Sorry, love, it's been . . .'

Her mother was crying. Lisa said, 'It's all right, Mum. That's terrific. Give him my love . . .' and then they were cut off.

'Wonderful news! Now you will sleep better,' Laurent said.

So Alice hadn't told about Lisa's nightmare. She must have said that Lisa couldn't sleep because she was worried about her grandfather. That was decent of her.

'Do you think if Grandpa's really better he'll be going home?' she asked Laurent.

'Not immediately. He has to be so that he doesn't need any of those machines. But soon he will be home again. Then we shall all go to see him,' Laurent said.

She didn't have to be anxious about Grandpa any more. But what about Elsbet? What about Alice?

She was grateful when the time came for her to go to school. She wouldn't have time to think there.

22

Everything seemed to be unwinding. It was nearing the end of term. It was April, and spring made a sudden, short visit, with a rush of pink blossom on the almond trees, buds everywhere, soft winds and loud blackbirds and robins. Then it was cold and windy again, but winter was definitely over. The evenings were light. Fanny came back from the country. Grandpa was coming out of hospital quite soon. Grandma wanted them to go to Lorrimer for Easter.

'You are too thin. I must feed you up,' Laurent said to Fanny.

'Cook me one of your marvellous casseroles. I feel as if I haven't seen real food for weeks.'

'Are you and Pierre getting on any better? I had a feeling you were,' Fanny said to Lisa. Lisa said, 'He's all right.' She didn't want to say any more. She didn't want to be asked about Alice. Not yet. Not until she knew herself what she felt.

The curious thing was that she and Alice seemed to be behaving exactly as they had before the night of the bad dream. They hardly spoke to each other. Alice wasn't ever in her half of the bedroom except to sleep, she still did her homework in her brother's room. But things had changed between Lisa and Pierre. On the day that they had heard the good news, he had said to her, 'I am happy that your Grandfather will be well.' And when Fanny had come back, Pierre had said, 'You are pleased to have your mother home again.'

Lisa was surprised into saying, 'Yes, I am. Aren't you?'

'I am pleased too. I think you are lucky.'

'Lucky? Me? Why?'

'You are lucky to have Fanny for your mother.'

Lisa remembered Fanny saying, 'You might be sorry for them. It can't be much fun discovering that your mother would rather not have you with her.' She said, 'Well, now you've got Fanny too.'

He hadn't answered that. But he had smiled. She had to admit that he had a nice smile. She had felt different about him since that conversation. But she still didn't know what she felt about Alice.

The school holidays began. But they weren't going to Lorrimer for Easter. 'It'd be too much for my father, he's still frail. And my mother's got enough to cope with,' Fanny said.

'But we should go away somewhere. Paris for a week?' Laurent suggested, but Fanny, with a quick look at Lisa, said, 'Let's go somewhere none of us has ever seen. It'd be more exciting.'

'So not Rome, now you have been there. Vienna?'

Lisa choked.

'What? Did you say something?' Laurent asked.

'I don't want to go to Vienna.'

'Why not? Everyone says it is beautiful. Mozart lived there. Schubert too. We could go to the riding school where they train the white horses. What is wrong with Vienna?'

She couldn't tell him the truth. 'I don't know. I just don't want to go there.'

'Where would you like to go, then? Amsterdam? I have been there, but none of the rest of you know it.'

Amsterdam. It reminded her of Anne Frank. 'No, not Amsterdam.'

'You suggest a place. Not too far away.'

Of course she couldn't think quickly of anywhere. She said, 'Couldn't we go somewhere warm, where we could swim?'

'In Greece the sea would be warm. Wouldn't it?' Pierre said.

'It is a four-hour plane journey to Greece. It would take too long and cost too much,' Laurent said.

'Anyway, I don't think the sea would be really warm yet,' Fanny said.

'What about Bruges? I hear it is pretty.'

No one seemed keen on Bruges.

'Then it seems that Vienna would be best. Lisa? What don't you like about it?'

She made herself say, 'It was horrible in the war.'

'Most places are horrible in a war. That is fifty years ago now.' Later, Fanny caught Lisa by herself. 'What's the reason why you don't want to go to Vienna, love?'

'It's because of Hitler and the Jews.'

'I shouldn't have told you about it,' Fanny said.

'Grandpa might have been killed there.'

'I know. But partly why I'd like to go there is to see the place where he grew up. I always think of him as English, but he lived in Vienna for the first twelve years of his life. I feel I've sort of missed out on that.'

So it was going to be Vienna. Laurent had found a hotel. He was booking their flights.

Lisa made one last effort to avoid it. 'Couldn't I go to stay with Grandma? I wouldn't be a nuisance. I could help.'

'No, you can't. Don't go on about it, Lisa.'

'Will I have to share a room with Alice?'

'Yes, you will. Separate rooms cost a lot more than doubles. It's only for three nights. Now go away and let me think what I'm doing.'

Vienna. The double mirror image. Elsbet.

Lisa didn't know what to do.

She wished that in the dream she had taken the kitten. She wished that she knew what had really happened to Elsbet. If she had died in the death camp, then Lisa couldn't do anything to help her. But suppose that because she'd been warned, as her brother Hans had been warned, she had somehow managed to escape? Suppose she had been hidden in someone's attic, like Anne Frank, and had never been discovered? She might be alive now. And if she wasn't, if she'd allowed herself to be carried off to the death camp, would that be Lisa's fault?

Lisa knew that she had to go back to try to talk to Elsbet once more.

It would be dangerous. She wasn't invisible in that dark room. Elsbet had seen her. If she was seen by one of Hitler's men, he would know that she was Jewish. Instead of rescuing someone else, she might find that it was she who was taken away to one of the death camps. 'But suppose I get killed in Vienna, what happens to me now? Would I die suddenly here? That's silly, what happens then can't make any difference to me now.' But it still felt dangerous. She did not want to go back again.

You can argue with yourself and find a hundred good reasons why you need not do something that is frightening, but if, underneath all the sensible excuses, you know with your most inside feelings that this is what you have got to do, in the end you find that you are doing it. Which is how it happened that on the morning of the day before they were due to leave for Vienna, Lisa was in Fanny's room once more, reluctantly turning her back on the big mirror on the wall and looking into the mirror in her hand.

She saw the same, high ceilinged room. Elsbet stood alone by the table, her eyes turned towards the open door, as if she expected someone to come in at any moment.

Lisa said, 'Elsbet!'

Elsbet looked towards her and said, 'You should go.'

'Listen! I've come back to tell you. You must escape. You must find somewhere to hide.'

'Why should I hide? This is a stupid game, I don't like it.'

'It's not a game! Hitler's soldiers . . . They'll come and take you away. They'll take you to the camps and kill you.'

'What camps? I don't understand. Why should the soldiers try to hurt me?'

'There's going to be a war . . .'

'If there is a war, our soldiers will be fighting the English, not us,' Elsbet said.

'It isn't the English who will kill you. It's Hitler. His soldiers. Because of you being Jewish. It's happening in Germany, now. Don't you know anything?' Lisa cried out.

'How do you know? You are not old enough to know anything,' Elsbet said.

'I know because I don't belong here. I've come back from another time, long after you, so I know what happened. It's history, I know about it.'

'How can you come back? You are trying to frighten me. You are pretending to be a ghost.'

'I'm not pretending anything. All right, then, I am a ghost!' If Grandma and Grandpa had thought she was a ghost, then perhaps that was what she was in this extraordinary world in which she didn't belong.

'My father says I should not let stupid people frighten me. You are only a boy. You don't know anything.'

'I'm not a boy. I'm a girl. And I do know,' Lisa said, angry.

'You are wearing boy's clothes. This is a trick. You are a bad boy to come here to try to make me afraid.'

Lisa opened her mouth to answer this silly, unbelieving little girl, but she never spoke. Something extraordinary was happening in the street outside. It wasn't, at first, a sound, it was the sudden stopping of sound. Before this she had just been aware of the ordinary noises below; of footsteps, of voices engaged in lively conversation, and the swish of car wheels and hooters. Now there was nothing, only a silence as if the people in the street below had suddenly been frozen so that they could neither walk nor talk.

The silence was broken at last by something new, the rhythmic stamp of boots. Hundreds of marching boots were approaching, echoing up from the road surface like a regular, menacing drum beat. And still, behind the clatter of metal on asphalt, was the silence. She knew that there must be people out there, watching this army of clattering feet. Why did no one speak? Why were there no voices to cheer the procession passing underneath these windows?

Then Lisa heard a voice. It was loud and it was harsh. It barked what sounded like an order and immediately the feet came to a clanging halt. A door below slammed suddenly with a crash that shook the whole house. There was the sound of heavy footsteps running up stairs. Feet in jackboots. The door was flung open and several soldiers burst into the room. Five or six men stood just inside the doorway. They had machine guns in their hands, as if they were ready to use them. In front of them was a young officer, very slim and straight in his black uniform, looking directly at Elsbet. He shouted a command and she stood up. The officer smiled. It was not an agreeable smile.

He asked her a question. It was in German. Lisa heard a word that sounded like 'father', and guessed that they were asking her where her father was.

Elsbet shook her head. The officer repeated the question. She shook her head again.

The young officer said something over his shoulder, and one of the men behind him came forward and took Elsbet by the shoulders. Another man levelled his gun at her head. The young officer asked the same question again.

This time Elsbet spoke. Lisa felt a sort of admiration for her. She was trembling and her eyes were huge with terror, but she managed to say something that apparently satisfied the officer. She was no longer held and the gun was directed away from her. The officer gave an order and the men behind him clattered off. From the noisy banging of doors and the sound of their boots, Lisa guessed that they had been ordered to search the other rooms in the apartment. The young officer remained standing, fixing Elsbet with his pale, expressionless gaze. She did not look at him, but down at the shining table.

One of the soldiers reappeared at the door. He asked a question. The young officer looked at him, then back at Elsbet, as if the answer concerned her. But at last he shook his head and turned towards the door. As he did so, he saw Lisa.

He spoke to her. She had no idea what he was saying. He motioned the soldier in the doorway, to lay hold of her. He said, '*Auch Juden*,' and Lisa somehow knew that he was saying that here was another Jewish child. Before the soldier could touch her, Lisa had stepped backwards towards the mirror. As she went, she saw a second soldier lift his machine gun and sweep the photographs off the tall cupboard on to the floor. The officer gave another order and the soldier was levelling his machine gun, pointed at her. She was being told to do something, to step forwards, to remain still, she didn't know what. She stepped back again just as the soldier fired. She heard the whine of the bullet as it passed over her head, she caught sight of Elsbet's face, her mouth open to scream. Then she was back in Fanny's bedroom, surrounded by light walls and silence. She was looking at the large mirror, with its surface damaged by that spider's web hole. She knew now when that had been made and how.

23

The city of Vienna was not at all as Lisa had imagined it. It was spacious and light and cheerful and some of it was indeed beautiful. The air was warm, there were flowers everywhere, people sat at little tables on the pavements outside cafes, eating and drinking. The shops were full of prettinesses. The cathedral of St Stefan was just what a cathedral should be, spired and patterned outside, dark and mysterious and richly smelling within. You couldn't forget for a moment that you weren't in England, you were 'abroad'.

But there had been a bad start. When they reached their hotel, they found that both the double rooms booked for them had double beds, in spite of the fact that Fanny had particularly insisted that one must have two singles. Fanny protested, the manager was called. He was desolate, but there was no way he could change the room. The hotel was full, so were all the other hotels in the city. 'Easter! What could he do?'

'I'm terribly sorry, but I'm afraid you'll just have to put up with it,' Fanny said to Alice and Lisa. She didn't know which of them might object most strongly.

To her surprise, they seemed to take it quietly. Fanny saw them look quickly at each other, but that was all. 'Almost as if they had a secret between them,' she said later to Laurent, who replied, 'I have begun to believe they might become friends.'

'Really? What makes you think that?'

'They are different with each other. They do not talk

much. But the way they look at each other is not as it was.'

It was true, they were still hardly on speaking terms. When they went to bed that first night, they lay as far apart as possible. It was a huge bed and there was quite a large space between them. Lisa lay awake for a time, listening to the unaccustomed sounds of Vienna beyond the window. Innumerable clocks striking the quarters and halves as well as the hours, feet on cobbles, voices shouting incomprehensible words, the distant murmur of cars, occasionally the clip-clop of a horse. Lisa had seen the horse-drawn carriages occupied by self-conscious tourists, driving around the old city.

She woke before Alice and found that during the night they had rolled towards each other. They were almost touching. She could smell Alice; the smell was a mixture of verbena shampoo, the same as she used, and of Alice herself. She realized that she had always taken for granted that she would hate Alice's smell. She would have said, if asked, that it would be fishy or stale or just rotten. Now that she was actually inhaling it, she found that it wasn't unpleasant. It was even comforting. Just as she thought this, Alice woke up, and they moved away from each other, still without speaking. But that morning, Lisa did not bother to hide herself in the bathroom before shedding her pyjamas to get dressed. That evening, she noticed, Alice changed for bed with the same lack of reserve.

It was a wonderful day. Vienna was much warmer than London. They had a midday meal sitting on the terrace of a restaurant high among the Vienna woods, from which they could see the city and the Danube – dirty grey, not blue at all – snaking around far below. A small orchestra played waltzes and marches, everyone there seemed happy. The food was unbelievably delicious, the sun shone. It couldn't have been less like the dark, dangerous place Lisa had imagined. In the afternoon they went down to explore the city; such grand buildings, such flowery parks, such magnificent churches. They strolled through the narrow streets of the old city, saw the house where Mozart had lived, visited the tiny museum that contained relics of his short life. They drank a hot sweet drink that tasted of real chocolate and not just of cocoa. Laurent bought bouquets for Fanny, Lisa and Alice, beautifully arranged tight nosegays of smaller flowers arranged round a central pink rose. 'Happy! I'm happy!' Lisa thought, surprised. It isn't often that you know that you are happy while the happiness is going on. It's more usual to think back afterwards and to say, 'Yes, I enjoyed that. That made me feel good.' Lisa was happy now, and knew it, perhaps because she hadn't expected to feel like this in Vienna.

It was late afternoon and they were all tired. Laurent suggested going back to the hotel for a short rest before they went out to find their evening meal, but Fanny objected. 'I want to see the place where my father lived when he was a boy. It was somewhere quite near the centre of the city. It can't be very far.'

'We could go tomorrow,' Laurent said.

'Remember we have to catch the afternoon plane, and that means getting to the airport hours before it takes off. I'd really rather go now, so that I don't feel rushed.'

'Do you want to go alone? Shall I take the children back to the hotel?'

'That's a good idea. I'll just go and have a look at the outside, then I'll join you.'

'Unless Lisa wants to go with you to see her grandfather's home,' Laurent said.

'Do you, Lisa?' Fanny asked.

Lisa didn't. She very much did not want to go to that street of marching feet, but she couldn't think of a good reason for refusing. She said, 'Yes, I'll go with you, Mum.' Perhaps they wouldn't be able to find it. In any case, it would probably look quite different now. 'I'll have to look at the street map. We're here . . . Rathausstrasse is there . . . I see. We have to go across the park. I don't think it'll take us more than ten minutes,' Fanny said, tracing their route with her finger on the street plan.

They crossed the park. Fanny was talking, but Lisa hardly heard what she said. In her mind she saw Grandpa walking along these paths, looking at these same trees and bushes. She saw him as a young boy, wearing those ridiculous knickerbockers and the jacket with a belt at the back. She herself had seen him in those clothes. She wondered what her mother would say if she was told that her daughter could describe the clothes her father had worn sixty years ago. She wouldn't believe it. Lisa could hardly believe it herself.

On the opposite side of the park, they crossed a wide road and entered a part of the city which was quite unlike anywhere they had been before. This was the Vienna that Lisa hadn't wanted to visit. She recognized the streets shadowed by the height and grey colour of the tall buildings surrounding them. They seemed to have left behind them the gaiety and the splendour of the old city; everything here was dark and grim. When Fanny said, 'Rathausstrasse. This is it,' Lisa recognized the street she had seen in her dream. She knew the doorway from which she had watched the passing crowd, and before Fanny had told her, she had said, 'This is where Grandpa lived, isn't it?'

'That's right! Clever girl! Their apartment was on the first floor. Let's go up and have a look.'

It wasn't easy for Fanny to explain what they wanted to the bustling woman in the cubicle just inside the heavy street door. Before she allowed them up the staircase, she had spoken on an internal telephone to someone else. They heard a door open in the house above and saw a young woman coming down the stairs towards them.

She said, '*Sie wollen* . . .?' then corrected herself. 'You are English? Maria does not understand.'

Fanny said, 'I'm so sorry to trouble you. My father lived

[127]

in this house when he was a little boy, and my daughter and I wanted just to look at it. I didn't mean to disturb you.'

'He lived here? Which apartment? You will forgive me, I speak so badly English.'

'No. You speak it very well. He lived on the first floor.'

'That is where I live. Why don't you come up to look? It would be interesting for you.'

So Lisa found herself standing again in the high ceilinged room with the tall narrow windows. But that was all that she recognized. The walls were white now, the furniture light and modern. There were children's toys on the low couch and on the floor. Only one or two pictures on the walls. No photographs, no mirror.

She was absorbed in remembering the room as it had been and she wasn't listening to the conversation between Fanny and their hostess until she heard Fanny say, sharply, 'No! Really? I thought everyone in the family had died. Except my father. He was in England when the war began.'

'This lady . . . she is Frau or Fräulein Rosen . . . somehow she escaped from going to the camp. It may have been from the train, I do not know. She hid somewhere and then she was in Poland, I think. Somehow she was never taken by the SS. I don't know how she lived in Poland. I think it was very hard for her.'

'But you say she's here now? In Vienna?'

'Yes. She came back here some years ago. She is living not far from here. I could find the address if you want.'

'But who is she? You said her name is Rosen. Was she Herr Rosen's sister? What relation was she?'

'I am afraid I don't know exactly. She could be a sister. No. She is not old enough. I think she said she lived here when she was a child.'

'But she was one of the family? Or did she marry one of the Rosens? Do you know her first name?'

'No, sadly I do not know it. But I may have it with her address. She came here one day, as you have come, to ask if she could look again because she had lived here. I wrote where she lives now. I have the paper somewhere.'

She went out of the room. Lisa said, 'Mum, it's Elsbet! Grandpa's sister. It must be. Don't you see?'

'You can't be sure. There may have been cousins with the same name. Friends, even. Rosen can't be a very uncommon name in Austria. And my father was told his sister had died in the camp.'

'But if she never went there? If she managed to stay hidden? It could be Elsbet.'

The young woman was back in the room. 'Yes, I have it. Fräulein Rosen. Here is the name of the street. It is not far from here.'

'Did she give you her first name?'

'She did not write it. She may have said. I do not remember. I am so sorry.'

'Do you know if she was here as part of a family? Did she have parents? A mother, a father?'

'Yes, I am sure. Because she said once, "This was Mutti's room." She said, also, something so that I thought she was not the only child. She said, "We were . . . scolded . . . because we shouted too loud." '

'Did she have a brother?'

'I do not know. Just, she said that. "We shouted." '

Fanny said, 'Thank you so much. You've been very kind. I'm glad to have seen the apartment. My father has described it to me, but that isn't the same as seeing it with my own eyes.'

'Please. If you want to come back I could show you all. The baby will be awake in the morning.'

In the street again, Fanny said, 'We'd better go now to this address she's given me. There won't be time tomorrow. Are you all right, love? It's quite near.'

'I'm all right. Who do you think she is, this Fräulein Rosen? Do you think it might be her? Grandpa's sister who was supposed to have been killed in the camp?'

'That's what we're going to find out. Oh, Dad! It'd be so wonderful for you if it really is your little sister . . .'

'Mum? If it really is Elsbet, it's good news. There's nothing to cry about.'

'No. I cry far more when people find each other after they've been separated than I do when they have to say goodbye.'

They had entered a street of small houses, with shops below the living quarters. It was a much poorer area than the one they had left. Fanny stopped in front of a shop selling fruit and vegetables.

'I wonder if I've got the number right? It doesn't look a likely place for an old lady to live.'

'But Elsbet isn't . . .'

'Isn't what?'

'Nothing.' Lisa had been on the point of saying, 'But Elsbet isn't an old lady, she's a little girl!' She had forgotten. Elsbet was an old lady. She was nearly as old as Grandpa.

A fat, middle-aged man, standing in the shop, asked them a question. Fanny shook her head. She asked, '*Sprechen sie Englisch*?' but of course the answer was, No. To gain time, she bought three oranges, and when the man was giving her the change, she asked, '*Fräulein Rosen*?'

He didn't seem to understand. He pointed to other fruit, other vegetables. He led the way inside the shop and waved a hand at the jars and tins on the shelves. Fanny repeated. '*Fräulein Rosen? Ist hier*?'

He scowled. He asked a question. Fanny couldn't answer it, she hadn't understood. She said again, '*Frälein Rosen*?'

Still scowling, he went to the back of the shop and opened a door. He leant through it and called. Neither Fanny nor Lisa could hear what name he called. There were steps coming slowly down stairs and along a passage. A woman came through the door, and the man said, '*Die Rosen*.'

She was old. She was bent with age. The pale skin of her scalp showed through between the strands of short grey hair. Her face was puckered with a thousand lines round a beak of a nose, underneath pouched, deep set eyes and a thin-lipped, bitter mouth. She was clutching a grey shawl round her shoulders, over a stained black dress. She said to the fat man, *'Was?'* and he jerked a thumb towards Fanny. He must have said, 'She asked for you.'

It can't be Elsbet! It isn't Elsbet! That dirty old woman can't be Grandpa's sister, Lisa thought. But Fanny was saying, 'Fräulein Rosen? Are you Fräulein Rosen?'

The old woman backed. She looked Fanny over suspiciously, almost with dislike. After a pause she said, 'You are English?'

'Yes, I'm English. Are you Elisabet Rosen?'

'Why do you ask? What is it to you?'

'I'm Fanny Rose. Hans . . . Johann Rose – Rosen – is my father. I think you are his sister. Aren't you Elsbet? Hans' sister?'

There was a long silence. Then the old woman said, 'Hans is alive?'

'Yes. He's alive and well.'

'He is living in England?'

'Yes. He is my father.' Fanny was not sure how much of what she had said this woman had understood.

'He sent you to find me?'

'No . . . not exactly. He does not know . . . He thought you had died.'

The woman laughed. 'It is convenient for him to say this. So he must not try to find me.'

'He was told that you died in the camp with your mother and father,' Fanny said.

'It was a lie. Everyone lies. How do I know you are speaking truth?'

'How would I know about Hans and Elsbet if I weren't Hans' daughter?'

The woman did not answer this.

Fanny said, 'Look . . . I'm going back to England

tomorrow, and I shall tell my father that we found you. I expect he will come here himself to see you, and to find out if there's anything we could do for you.'

'He will not come.'

'Not at once. He's been very ill. But as soon as he's better, I know he'll want to find you again.'

'He will not come. He could have come before so many years.'

'He did! He tried to find you after the war. But no one could tell him anything about you. He thought you had died with your mother and father.'

'He will not come again.'

'As soon as he's well again, he will.'

'Many people pretend illness so they must not do what they should.'

Fanny had begun to answer this, when the woman's glance slid to Lisa, standing behind her mother. She said urgently, 'Who is that child?'

'That's Lisa. My daughter. Hans is her grandfather.'

'She cannot be real. She is a ghost. Take her away.'

'I don't understand. What do you mean?'

Elsbet said, 'That child is not alive. It is a dead child you have with you. You should be careful.'

Fanny put out a hand for Lisa's and held it tightly. She said to Elsbet, 'We have to go now. But you can be sure I shall tell my father about you and that as soon as he can he will come here.'

Elsbet stepped forward. She was shrieking. 'Go away! I do not know you! My brother is dead. All are dead. Soon I shall be dead too, *gottwillen* . . .' The fat man turned on her and spoke in German. Fanny did not understand what he said, but she knew that it was an order, roughly given. He had raised an arm as if to strike. Fanny called out, 'Don't hit her!' and Elsbet shrank back. She shot out one last incomprehensible word at Fanny and disappeared through the door she had come in by.

[132]

'*Sehen sie? Die Alte ist blöd. Krank,*' he said.

'I don't understand,' Fanny said. Lisa could feel her trembling.

'Crazy. *Ist* crazy.'

Fanny backed out of the shop, still clutching Lisa. She said to the fat man, 'Don't hurt her.' He did not answer.

Fanny and Lisa walked hand in hand along the narrow pavement. Lisa saw tears running down her mother's face. She said, 'Mum?'

'I'm sorry you had to see that,' Fanny said.

'Do you think that really was Elsbet?'

'I don't know. I'd like not to think so. But I'm afraid it probably is.'

'Were you frightened?'

'Yes, I was. Weren't you?'

'I thought she was going to hit you or something.'

'Whatever she's been through, it's made her very bitter.'

'Do you think she is crazy, like that horrible man said?'

'I think probably. I don't see why she should turn against her own brother like that if she was in her right mind.'

'She didn't believe you,' Lisa said.

'Don't be frightened of what she said, love. Crazy people have crazy ideas. I don't know why she didn't think you were real.'

'Because she'd seen me when she was a little girl. I was a ghost to her then,' Lisa thought. She said, 'It was Elsbet, Mum. I'm sure.'

'Why are you sure?'

It was Lisa's turn to say, 'I don't know.'

'She's a poor old thing. And she certainly seems crazy. But I can't forget that she was my father's little sister. I don't know what we can do about her. I'll have to talk to Grandpa. And Laurent,' Fanny said. Tears were still running down her cheeks. Lisa pressed the hand she was still holding. 'I do understand, Mum. Don't worry.'

The rest of the evening became, for Lisa, a sort of blur.

Fanny wasn't fit to go out for the celebratory last meal they'd planned, she couldn't stop crying. And to Lisa's surprise, Pierre and Alice understood, without being told the reason, why they should instead get a sort of picnic meal to eat in their rooms. Laurent supervised their hastily improvised supper; rolls filled with ham and cheese, a delicious winey drink, chocolate cake. But Lisa wasn't hungry. And when Pierre asked her 'Do you feel well? You haven't eaten,' she said, 'I can't,' and was grateful that he didn't ask why.

In bed that night, after the light had been turned off, Lisa lay in the huge bed and remembered the voice of the old, shabby woman saying 'It is a dead child you have with you . . .' It wasn't frightening that she had been called a dead child. Lisa understood that. It was horrifying that the child Elsbet, who had hugged the kitten and who had loved Hans and Evelyn, should have become this miserable, hating old witch. Lisa sniffed.

'Lisa?' Alice said.

'I'm all right,' Lisa lied.

'You should tell me. I won't tell anyone.'

'Nothing to tell.'

'Fanny and you. Something bad happened to you today. Tell me.'

'I can't.'

'I saw Fanny crying. If it is bad, you should cry too.'

Lisa did not want to cry. She did not want to let Alice into this world that belonged to her family.

'When I knew that we were not to see my mother again, I tried not to cry. I wanted to be a brave person. But my father told me, "Cry, make a fuss. Feelings are real. If you pretend that you don't feel, you are killing something inside you." He said, "Cry!" '

'Did you cry?'

'I cried for days. Not all the time. But when I had to.'

'Did you mind so much about your mother? I thought . . .'

Alice said, carefully, 'It wasn't as it would have been with

[134]

Fanny. Your mother. She was not with us as your mother is. She was always too busy. I think I would have liked it if she had been sorry that we were going away. That was why I cried.'

Lisa said, 'We saw Elsbet. She was my grandpa's little sister who he thought was dead.' But when she had said this, she did begin to cry and she couldn't speak.

'So what will your grandfather do? Will he come here to fetch her to England?'

'I don't know.' Tears poured out of Lisa's eyes as she thought of what her grandfather would feel when he saw the bitter, dirty old woman that his little sister had become.

'You should go to sleep now. It is late.'

'I'm too wide awake. I won't be able to go to sleep.'

'I shall stroke your neck, then you will sleep.'

Surprisingly, after a time, Lisa did.

24

They had been back in London for a day before Lisa asked her mother, 'Have you told Grandpa about . . . Elsbet?'

'No. I wanted to wait till he's back home. He can't do anything about her until he's quite strong again.'

'Do you think he will go over to fetch her?'

'I'm sure he'll want to go to see her. But she may not want to come back with him.'

'It'll be horrible for him. Seeing her like that.'

'That's another reason for waiting till he's better.'

Lisa's grandfather was better surprisingly soon. Before the summer school term had started, he was out of hospital and back at Lorrimer. 'You must all come and stay here for half term, and we'll have a party to celebrate,' Lisa's grandmother wrote.

'That's a wonderful idea. The weather might be really good by the end of May,' Fanny said.

'Not if it goes on like it is now. I'm cold!' Lisa said, outraged that when the calendar said it was summer, the wind should be chilly, bringing a small, spiteful rain.

It went on being cold until halfway through the month, when suddenly everything changed. The sun shone and it was warm, even hot. There were flowers everywhere, exuberant pink and white flowers on rhododendron bushes, bunches of clotted white pear blossom in the next door garden, spiked white and red candles on the chestnut trees. It was wonderful to be able to go out into the street in a thin shirt and to feel warm air on the face and arms. Lisa longed to be at Lorrimer. She wanted most of all to see her grandparents, but she wanted, too, to see the garden and the country around. It was the time of year to be out of a town, and to be able to look at fields and hills and woods and streams.

She asked Fanny again, 'Have you told Grandpa about . . . his sister?'

'Not yet. I thought it would be better to wait till I'm with him. I don't want to have to say it over the telephone.'

Lisa couldn't get Elsbet out of her mind. She couldn't imagine how Grandpa would feel if he was expecting to see his little sister as she had been before the war, and then he saw that old, old woman who wouldn't believe that he had wanted to find her. She worried about it. She wondered whether Elsbet would come to believe that he had thought she was dead. Suppose he and Grandma asked her to come and live at Lorrimer and she agreed? It would spoil the place for everyone. But Grandpa certainly wouldn't allow her to go on living in the horrible shop with the disagreeable fat man ordering her about. The more Lisa thought about it, the more worried she became.

She was still more anxious when they all arrived at the house in the last week of May. The garden and the country around were just as beautiful as she had imagined, but she couldn't be quite easy until she knew that Fanny had told her father what they had discovered in Vienna. She thought back to the last time they had all been there together. That had been last Christmas, and she had been angry because she had to share a room with Alice. Now that didn't bother her. She wasn't sure she didn't even quite like having someone to talk to after they'd gone to bed. Somehow when it was dark, it was easier to say things that you wouldn't feel like telling if you'd been able to see the face of the person you were talking to. Which was how it happened that on their fourth night at Lorrimer, Lisa told Alice about Elsbet.

She couldn't, of course, tell her that she'd seen Elsbet as a little girl. But she did tell her that Elsbet was now an old woman and how horrible she had been. 'She thinks Grandpa just didn't bother to find out what had happened to her. She talked as if she hated him.'

'That is why you have been unhappy?'

'I'm not exactly unhappy.'

'But you are worried.'

'If he goes to see her and she's horrible to him, it'll be so dreadful for him. I'm sure he still thinks of her as his little sister.'

'Did he love her very much?'

'Mum thinks he did.' Lisa had to be careful not to know too much about Hans and Elsbet when they were children.

'Then why is she hating him now? I would not hate Pierre, whatever he did.'

'Mum thinks it was what happened to her in the war. She thinks she must have been badly treated and it made her like she is. She's sort of mad. She screams at people, and . . .' But Lisa couldn't bring herself to tell Alice that Elsbet was dirty. Though she hadn't liked her, that would have seemed like betraying her.

Soon after this conversation, Fanny said to Lisa, 'I've told Grandpa about Elsbet.'

'What . . .? What did you say about her?'

'Not much. Only that she wasn't killed in the camp where his parents died and that we'd seen her in Vienna.'

'You didn't tell him what she's like?'

'I couldn't. It was upsetting enough just to know that she was alive.'

'Didn't he ask what she looks like? What she said about him?'

'No. I think it was such a shock to hear about her, that was all he could take in. Of course I said I'd told her that we'd come back and try to look after her.'

'Mum! It's going to be terrible for Grandpa when he sees her.'

'I know. But something will have to be done about her. We can't leave her there. Grandpa isn't going to be well enough to go to Vienna for some time yet. I think I might have to go back myself, to see what can be done.'

'You mean, bring her back here?'

'Or arrange for her to live somewhere decent and be properly looked after there. I'm not at all sure she'd agree to come over here.'

'I hope she doesn't.'

'I'm afraid I do, too.'

Lisa was frightened that her grandfather might ask her about Elsbet. She had no idea what she could say that wouldn't be upsetting. She was glad that when they were together he never mentioned Elsbet's name.

When she was back in London, in the middle of the summer term, she didn't have much time for thinking about the Elsbet problem. But one day, finding herself alone in Fanny's bedroom in the late afternoon, she looked at the big looking glass and shivered. The spider's web fracture reminded her of her last sight of the child Elsbet, the soldiers in the high ceilinged room, which she had now seen in real life. She thought, 'But that room was real, too. I saw Elsbet there, I was talking to her. The mirror was broken then, it's still got the mark. If I went back again, could I tell Elsbet that Grandpa believed she was dead and that's why he didn't go to look for her?'

She picked up the hand mirror and turned her back on the long looking glass. She wasn't sure that she was brave enough to go back again into the dark world to which it led. It took a moment or two before she dared to look at its reflection in the mirror she held in her hand.

But the hand mirror did not reflect the Viennese room, nor the room in London where she had seen Hans and Evelyn. Instead she saw her mother's bedroom, exactly as it was when she raised her eyes and looked at the real thing instead of the reflection of a reflection.

It was instant relief. So she could not go back to that dangerous apartment in Vienna, even if she had wanted to.

The relief did not last. When she looked again at the reflection of Fanny's room, she saw what should not have been there.

There was a figure between her and the dressing table. She turned sharply, with a cold stab of fear, and saw no one. But when she looked back at the double reflection, she saw the figure again and knew that it was the old woman who had been Elsbet.

Lisa's dry mouth managed to say, 'How . . .? I thought you were in Vienna. My mother was going to go out there to see you.'

'I am not in Vienna.'

'How did you get here?'

'I came through the door.' Lisa looked at the door of her mother's room and the old woman gave a scornful laugh. 'Not that door. The door you came through. The mirror.'

Lisa remembered Pierre's saying, 'Mirrors are doors for Death to enter.' She said, 'When I came through the mirror, everyone thought I was a ghost. You said I must be a ghost.'

'That is right. Only ghosts can go through such doors.'

'But I'm alive. You're alive. I saw you. In Vienna.'

'That was yesterday.'

'It was weeks ago!'

'You have no idea of time. Today I am not alive.' Lisa said, 'I don't see . . .'

'You don't have to see. I have to say it quickly, I have not long here. I came to say that I understand about Hansi. It was you who told him so that he was saved. I know that he did come to look for me. In Vienna I did not know this.'

'I don't understand!' Lisa cried out and saw the old woman frown as she said, 'Then you are stupid. *Dummkopf.*'

'I'm not! You don't explain!' Lisa said, and turned to look directly into the big mirror. Her eyes caught the faintest hint of a flicker between her and the glass. Then there was nothing.

She looked back into the double reflection in the hand mirror. She saw the pale empty room. She was alone.

'If I hadn't gone back and warned Elsbet, would she have been taken to the camp and died?' she wondered. And wondered, too, whether it was worse to die as a child, still able to love and be loved, or to escape death then, if the rest of your life made you bitter and hating. She, Lisa, had meant to help. Had she really made everything worse? 'But next time I see Grandpa, I can tell him that Elsbet understood about him in the end. She knew that he never forgot her,' Lisa thought.

'I'm going to be away this weekend. Think you can manage?' Fanny said at breakfast a day or two later.

'You think we are helpless without you?' Laurent asked.

'Where are you going, Mum? To see Grandpa?'

'I'm going back to Vienna.'

'What for? Why?'

'I feel I should try to see Grandpa's sister again. He's not going to be well enough this summer.'

'But Mum!'

'What?'

'She's . . . Suppose she's died?'

'Why should she have died? If she had, that man should have let me know. I left my address with him.'

Laurent said, 'If she comes back with you, it is going to be a shock for your father.'

'I know. But what else can I do?'

'Will he not be pleased to know about his sister?' Pierre asked.

'She has changed a great deal since he saw her last.'

'I would be pleased to see Alice. Unless she was contradicting me like she often does.'

'No, I don't!'

'What are you doing now, then, I should like to know?'

'Be quiet, you two. This poor woman has suffered terribly. Fanny says that she is a little mad. She is not the same person that Fanny's father knew when she was a little girl,' Laurent said.

But Fanny did not go to Vienna.

'Lisa. I wanted to tell you. I heard today. Grandpa's sister died last week.'

Lisa said, 'Yes.'

'You don't sound very surprised,' Fanny said.

'I am really. So Grandpa won't have to know about her?'

'I think he could be told that we saw her and that she was ill. I don't have to tell him everything she said.'

'She was crazy. Wasn't she, Mum?'

'I think so, yes. I don't know what she'd been through, but it must have been more than she could take. Don't cry, Lisa. It really isn't anything to do with you.'

'I'd sort of thought . . .'

'What, love?'

'I'd thought how pleased Grandpa would be if she came back again. If she'd been like she was before. After he'd given her up for dead. It would have been like . . . like the end of *Traviata*. You know. Armand and Marguerite finding that they'd really loved each other all the time.'

'If it had been like that . . . I agree, it would have been wonderful.'

'I wanted to see them together.' Lisa couldn't say that she'd hoped to be the person who had made the meeting possible.

'But considering what she'd become I'm thankful he isn't going to see her.'

'He'll be sad to know that she is really dead, won't he?'

'I think what will be saddest for him is to feel that she was alive all those years and he didn't know it.'

'Mum? Could he have found her before now?'

'He tried. He told me he'd done everything he could to

[142]

trace her. But then he was told definitely that she'd died in the camp, and that made him stop looking.'

'If Alice was lost, somehow, you'd look for her, wouldn't you?' Lisa asked Pierre.

'Lost how? How do you mean, lost?'

'If you hadn't seen her for years and you didn't know where she was.'

'You are thinking of your grandfather and his sister.'

'Yes.'

'Of course I would look. I would miss her. I am sure your grandfather missed his sister too.'

'And she'd look for you.'

'She might.'

'You're lucky, you and Alice. I wish I had a sister. Or a brother.'

'You have us,' Pierre said.

'If I was lost, would you look for me?'

He pretended to consider. 'Perhaps I would. It would depend on how rude you had been to me just before you were lost. If you had called me Frog, I would let you stay away.'

'I've never called you Frog!'

'You wanted to. When we were first here.'

'That was a long time ago,' Lisa said.

FABER CHILDREN'S CLASSICS

The Children of Green Knowe
by Lucy Boston

The River at Green Knowe
by Lucy Boston

The Mouse and His Child
by Russell Hoban

Marianne Dreams
by Catherine Storr

The Mirror Image Ghost
by Catherine Storr

Make Lemonade
by Virginia Euwer Wolff